cruel summer

cruel summer
kylie adams

the first novel in the
fast girls,
hot boys
series

POCKET BOOKS   MTV BOOKS

New York   London   Toronto   Sydney

POCKET BOOKS, a division of Simon & Schuster, Inc.
1230 Avenue of the Americas, New York, NY 10020

ISBN-13: 978-1-4165-2032-0
ISBN-10:   1-4165-2032-5

This MTV Books/Pocket Books trade paperback edition March 2006

10 9 8 7 6 5 4 3 2 1

Manufactured in the United States of America

For information regarding special discounts for bulk purchases, please contactSimon & Schuster Special Sales at 1-800-456-6798 or business@simonandschuster.com

For Karen Thorne,
the best astrologist a neurotic writer
could ask for!

You can be rich and not be famous.
You could be famous and not be rich.
But to be rich and famous is a
special category all by itself.

—Kimora Lee Simmons

cruel summer

From: Bijou

OMG—there's blood everywhere!

10:05 pm 5/26/06

prologue

he seat was empty.

Unbelievably empty. Heartbreakingly empty. Shockingly empty.

Just one more example of cold, hard proof. Beyond the media coverage, the tears, and the funeral. Proof that a young life had been violently snuffed out before its time.

Bijou Ross approached the podium. She looked out at the audience assembled in the auditorium of the Miami Academy for Creative and Performing Arts.

The audience gazed back at her.

Bijou could feel their anticipation rising, and as the expectant silence boomed, her heartbeat accelerated, pumping hard, leaping around in her chest. The look on her face said she was worried about what words to use.

Here she was—valedictorian, class of 2006. They were waiting for her to communicate. They wanted a speech. They needed some insight. From the girl who'd gotten a literary agent and a book deal months before her cap and gown. Hopes were pinned on her to provide some verbal balm for their souls, to make sense of the insensible. Yet Bijou, the one billed in the yearbook as "most likely to win a Pulitzer," just stood there with writer's block. The irony seemed lost on no one.

It was still morning-after-the-hurricane. The murder so fresh in their minds that ears were still ringing from the gunshot. To throw out platitudes for the future would only be wasted breath. They'd all been to the same party, witnessed the same unbelievable act, seen the same pool of blood, heard the same dying declarations. From someone just like them. Young, blessed with talent, and with everything to live for.

Bijou knew this much: The trauma would stay with them. Years from now the pain would linger in dark places, and even as adults, they'd never be quite free of it. Because one of their own had stopped breathing in front of their eyes. And the memory of that would cling forever.

Peering down from the lectern, Bijou found them. Somewhere in the vast crowd. For a moment, her mind plunged into a happier place. The image was technicolor vivid. A Saturday on South Beach. So early that the morning light was crystal white. Bijou had been there to bask in the solitude, to walk on the caramel sand, to think through a plot puzzle for her book.

And they'd been there, too. Vanity, Dante, Max, Pippa, and Christina. Strolling along the edge of the surf, drinking thimblefuls of Cuban coffee from David's Café, their minds lost in iPod sounds. Oh, yes. The school's Fabulous Five.

A mist began to build in Bijou's eyes. There was no way she could continue looking at them and still maintain her composure. As she averted her gaze, a decision was made. That would be the picture seared into her brain to remember them by. The snapshot of all five.

But now there were only four.

Anxiety began to build. Bijou could feel the tension. The mournful silence had stretched on too long. Attention was gridlocked onto her. And she had to get on with it now. From somewhere she would have to dig up the phrases. To find the words that possessed the virtue of both simplicity and sincerity.

Finally, Bijou began to speak, and miraculously, the voice she heard was full of vibrant reassurance. "My fellow graduates, it is a sad day for all of us . . ."

From: Mimi

You MUST hit Mynt tonight. Lohan is out of
control. Come. Be your gorgeous self.
Upstage the bitch.

11:03 pm 6/17/05

chapter one

Vanity St. John patrolled the velvet rope of Black Sand like a child of Hitler. It was the hot club of the millisecond. She was the hot girl of the moment. A match made in flashbulb heaven.

For fistfuls of cash she didn't need and a VVIP membership she didn't want, Vanity had agreed to this two-hour promotional stunt. So here she was playing Celebrity Rope Bitch.

Three guys inched forward to beg entry.

One glance and Vanity knew. Wrong look. Wrong zip

code. Wrong everything. With Gestapo precision, she waved them out of the line.

"Yo! What's up?" The leader of the loser pack had spoken.

Vanity ignored him. She was good at that. Rendering people invisible came easy. Someone in the next gaggle of hopefuls brought a hint of a smile to her glossy lips.

He loped toward her, cockier than Usher on the red carpet. "Hey, baby. I haven't seen you since that Gap thing." Jayson James was talking.

Vanity St. John was remembering. Last spring's print campaign. The male model with the California surfer vibe. The postshoot date that ended with them half-drunk but all over each other in the limousine. And the promised call that never materialized. Ooh, a guy who pulls a disappearing act after a hookup. How original.

She noticed the initials J.J. tattooed onto the underside of his left wrist. Oh, yeah. The nickname. It all came flooding back now. This was the corn-fed stud from Iowa. Discovered in Times Square during a senior trip to New York. His West Coast beach dude act was just a pathetic attempt at reinvention. It played better with bookers and advertising creative types.

J.J.'s beautiful baby blues flicked her up and down. No doubt the memory of what they did together was stripping the gears of his one-track mind. But dumb guys could only think so much. Especially a Midwest moron like him. If this one ever needed brain surgery, the doctor would have to say, "Okay, nurse, unzip his pants."

"I just got a J. Crew shoot in the Hamptons for next week," he said, flashing her a hopeful look through hooded, lust-filled eyes. "Any chance I'll see you there?"

"Sorry," Vanity sniffed. "I don't do catalog work. Anyway, I'm booked up with D and G." She unhooked the velvet rope to offer him the A-list access he craved . . . just as her subtle dig that he was strictly B-grade hit the jasmine-drenched ether of the steamy Miami night.

The frozen expression on J.J.'s face told her that his farm boy mind was tilling the verbal land, trying to determine whether or not he'd just been slammed. Backbreaking work for him. In fact, he already needed a lunch break. Yes, the guy was hot. His Hilfiger boxer brief underwear ads had proven that. But sitting next to him on a long flight? That could possibly kill a girl with boredom.

The other two members of his posse—a dead ringer who had to be J.J.'s brother and a tragic blonde who needed to introduce herself to Proactiv Solution—scooted fast to join him on the other side. God, what a lame crew. Hardly a hand-picked entourage. More like an accidental cluster. J.J. better watch out. By this time next year he could be modeling for International Male and be lucky to have the gig.

Vanity waited for them to pass through, then rehooked the rope with a loud clink of doom.

"Stuck-up bitch!"

She whipped her head around. It was the first group again. Please. Shouldn't they be back on a bus by now? This was typical, though. It didn't matter if they were rich, poor, or somewhere in the middle. Latin guys had a tough time with rejection. Vanity had dated and discarded enough of them to know. She blamed their mothers. Too much coddling.

"You let them in! Why not us?" It was the kind of whining you might hear from a little boy who didn't get chosen for a game of pickup basketball.

"Oh, now that's sexy," Vanity cooed with mock breathiness, rolling her eyes skyward.

The crowd within earshot laughed.

This only pissed off the guy more. He grabbed his crotch and yelled, *"Puta barata!"*

Vanity wasn't bilingual, but she knew enough Spanish to understand that he was calling her a cheap whore. Her eyes flashed fire. *"Retrasado,"* she hissed. The only Spanish word she could think of. But it suited him perfectly. English translation: retard.

All of a sudden, Vanity felt guilty, realizing that these idiots didn't know any better. So she stalked toward them to deliver a lesson in style. Nothing like a little bit of charity work to ease a girl's conscience.

"You should know better than to show up in shorts and Nike tees," Vanity barked. "And please—get rid of the gold chains."

That was all she had the heart to say. How could she tell them the truth? That even if they turned out head-to-toe in cutting-edge Prada, their chance of getting past the rope was still slim to none. Some people just didn't have *the look*. Too bad. So sad.

It was Friday night in South Beach. The clock had ticked past midnight. But Cinderella was *not* going home. In fact, she was just getting started.

Vanity felt a surge of uninhibited energy. Here, on Collins Avenue, the young warriors were out and ready to fight for their right to party. They were queued up, trailing at least hundreds deep, an endless line of blazing color, burning impatience, and sweating desperation. To get in. To be seen. To do social damage.

And Vanity St. John was the door police. The all-powerful gatekeeper. With one crook of her freshly manicured finger she could make someone's night . . . or break it. She gave two Black Sand bouncers the signal. It was time for the clean sweep.

This part could get ugly. That's why the incredible hulks flanked her on each side, their arms out wide to separate the teen celebutante from the throng of potential club animals steaming up the sidewalk. Their hunger was palpable. They wanted to get on the right side of the red rope. As badly as they wanted to breathe.

Vanity strutted down the gauntlet.

Dumb and Dumber huffed and puffed to keep up with her.

She glanced over the crowd, sizing them up, sorting them out. What a motley crew. And she didn't mean the bad heavy metal band that wouldn't go away. If nightlife hounds were walking slabs on their way to the meat market, then bacon was the only choice here. No prime rib within sight.

Vanity managed a patiently polite vibe as she dismissed almost all of them. The nervous. The ugly. The too old. The tourists. The fashion tragedies. But throughout her cold-water-cool process of elimination, she experienced real pangs of sympathy.

If Vanity's own gene pool (music mogul father, ex-supermodel mother) hadn't been so extraordinary, then she might've been just like them. Always segregated from the Beautiful People. Always reminded that she wasn't quite good enough to join the VIP party. Maybe she'd be happier that way, though. After all, phenomenal looks didn't exactly guarantee a phenomenal life. And she was living proof of that.

But Vanity pressed on, passing over a barbershop quartet of fraternity boys. Way too bland. They were sports bar ready, not Black Sand worthy.

"Hey, come on! My uncle's a producer! We're on the list!"

Vanity regarded the rude one. A Phi Delta Theta with too many Bud Lights on the brain. Mildly cute at best. The kind of Abercrombie mall rat who gets hired during the holiday rush, when the standards are low and the need for warm bodies is high. Somebody had to fold the sweaters.

She made this assessment in less than a blink. By comparison, a nanosecond was a long day. So to the untrained eye, Vanity didn't so much as twitch a muscle in response.

And then she saw him. A real scene seeker who knew how to accessorize. Only he didn't do it with bad jewelry. He did it with sculpted muscle. Wearing destroyed-wash True Religion jeans and a ribbed Calvin Klein wife beater, this boy could only do Black Sand good. In a perfect world, the Von Dutch belt buckle would be history. But Vanity forgave him this slight miscue because the razor cuts of his deltoids more than made up for it.

She waved him up to the lip of the party landslide.

Some boys were hot. This one was on fire. Definitely stop-and-stare gorgeous. Obviously of mixed race, too. His skin color captivated her. Vanity guessed Puerto Rican father and black mother. Or maybe the reverse. But of this she could be sure: He was the exact hue of Cuban coffee after adding warm milk. The tuft of hair on his chin jutted out like an exclamation point. If she had to compare, he was a young Lenny Kravitz without the pincushion piercings, save for the single cubic zirconia gleaming from one ear.

"I think you belong in there," she said, pointing to the steel door that, at least right here and right now, seemed to be the pathway that proved desirability as a human being.

The chosen one hesitated. "What about my friend?"

Vanity turned to see a tall black guy skulking a few feet behind—jeans hanging off his ass, Allen Iverson jersey, Timberland boots. Standard issue. Nothing special. But on a busy night he stood a fifty-fifty chance of getting in. "Sorry." She said no because she could. "You'll have to watch him on the dis cam."

Black Sand was famous for its big-screen television with closed-circuit video honed in on the unfortunates trapped outside.

The buddy took the bad news in stride. "I'm gonna roll, man. Peace." He flashed the eternal symbol.

His luckier friend didn't echo the gesture. "Hold up, Vince." Then he looked at Vanity. "Listen, if my boy can't come, too, then we're out of here."

"How loyal," Vanity sniffed. "What are you—a golden retriever?" But even as she mocked the gesture, she secretly admired him for sticking by his friend.

He ignored her question and asked his own. "Aren't you a model or something?"

Model. As Vanity heard it, the word fell off his pretty lips with the subtle hint that this didn't exactly top his list of impressive jobs. "I'm more of a *personality,*" she explained in the dense tone usually reserved for a clueless tourist asking for directions.

"And what does a *personality* do?" he asked. But before she could answer, he added, "Besides model."

The bad noun had become a bad verb. Wow. Clever semantics. In answer, Vanity peered down at him with a haughty glare. She stood at least an inch taller in her Manolo Blahnik heels. The look on her face said quite clearly, "You probably crossed the river from Little Havana to get here. So ask me if I care what you think about models."

And then she noticed the tattoo on his left arm. While J.J. chose to ink his stupid nickname, this boy had serious things to say with body art. It was a tribute to someone: L. MEDINA. Complete with birth and death dates and navy rank and serial number. The life span told her that it could be his father, and if so, that he'd lost him at a very young age.

"My dad," he confirmed, picking up on her curiosity. "He died in Desert Storm." His voice got caught. And there was real emotion in the eyes that shone like two black infinity pools.

Right away Vanity felt bad for the private rant. For a moment, she studied the ground, uncertain how to respond. Suddenly, her palms began to sweat and her heart picked up speed. God, what was happening? Guys weren't supposed to do this to her. She was supposed to do it to them.

But this boy was different. He dealt in deep ends. And that put him in another category. Already it seemed like their little spat about his model crack happened a million years ago.

Fear of silence wasn't a problem for him. He didn't just steal a glance. He stood there and openly checked her out. Those dark eyes sparkled at her.

Vanity's emerald green ones sparkled right back. She shook out her long, panther black hair that was flat-ironed to perfection, just as she threw a leg forward to set the best angle of her body. There was pretty. There was beautiful. And there was impossibly gorgeous. She belonged in the rarified orbit of number three. And she knew it.

With a wildly colorful Pucci scarf wrapped over modest breasts and knotted in the back to create an instant halter and glitter gold hot pants drawing a dangerous line between thigh and butt cheek, Vanity was state-of-the-trend. In Miami, bare skin ruled. Homes were where you slept, gyms were where you lived, and indecent exposure fines were only slapped on those whose bodies should be covered up. Vanity's ensemble tonight was her signature look. Seventeen and dressed to kill grown men. So why wasn't the boy in front of her dead yet?

"I'm sorry," Vanity said, suddenly realizing that the bit about his father was still hanging in the air.

He shrugged off the memory. "It was a long time ago."

But Vanity could sense the pain of the loss tugging at him right now. She wanted to tell him that she knew what it was like. To come straight off the assembly line from the Wounded Childhood Factory. Her own father was still alive, but as a parent, he might as well have been six feet under. That's how little he cared. Sure, Simon St. John was a music industry legend. His office walls were covered floor-to-ceiling with platinum records. But on the family front, Daddy Dearest didn't just hit some bad notes. The man bombed miserably.

"I'm Dante Medina." He put out his hand to her.

She accepted it, her hand melting into his. "Vanity St. John."

He squeezed. There was poetry in the pressure. And his touch lingered long enough to matter. "You're Simon St. John's daughter?"

She nodded, pursing high-gloss lips steel-trap tight. Where did this guy come from? Okay, so the sperm donor responsible for her first breath knew the recording business. But in the great American fame game, he was Vanity St. John's father more than anything else. She had the first-class modeling assignments, the endorsement deals, the paparazzi chronicling her every move for *Us Weekly,* the book editors burning up the wire to publish everything from her diaries to her shopping lists.

Dante smiled. His amazing eyes were probing. The look on the face that would haunt her dreams tonight told her that he knew something that she didn't. "Chances are I'll see you around," he said before sloping off, signaling his friend to follow.

Vanity watched them disappear through the steel door that led to Black Sand and its monster-length bar, its mammoth dance floor, and its private rooms where wonderfully terrible behavior went on until five in the morning.

As Dante slipped through the coveted entrance, the raging music from inside charged into the hot South Beach night. The wicked cut "Don't Phunk with My Heart" by Black Eyed Peas enlivened the outside crowd for the few seconds they were lucky enough to hear it.

When Vanity woke up this morning, her world had been

chockablock full of guys like J.J. the model. Typical red-blooded males who ran on the adrenaline of beer binges and sex schemes. But Dante Medina was something else entirely. As his name roamed around in her mind, the butterflies flew loose in her stomach.

And Vanity sensed a powerful feeling that her life had just changed.

From: Pippa

I'm wearing my best pair of underwear tonight.
Guess which color.

11:23 pm 6/17/05

chapter two

On Max Biaggi Jr.'s planet, speed limits were for kids who financed used cars with fast-food paychecks.

His Puma-clad foot leaned heavily on the Porsche 911 accelerator.

Varoom!

The twin-turbo, flat-six engine roared. Oh, damn, could this baby fly. Like a sleek black rocket in blast-off mode.

Blink. The speedometer went triple digit. Just that quick. He redlined it in every gear along the MacArthur Causeway. The moon was shining. The Biscayne Bay breeze was blowing. The party was waiting. In Miami. A place where nights were *not* for sleeping.

Thump-thump-thump went Ciara's "One, Two Step,"

blasting so loud from twelve Bose speakers that it drowned out the 444-horsepower revs. So what if the track had pumped hard more than a year ago? It was after midnight in South Beach. And a sick Missy Elliott groove was more sacred than gospel music.

All of a sudden, blue lights flashed in the rearview mirror. Then a blistering siren screamed over the infectious crunk jam.

Oh, shit. For a moment, Max's heart stopped beating. Like he needed another ticket. Or another DUI. He pulled over to the side, popped a chicklet of cinnamon gum, and got his driver's license ready for inspection.

The cop was a bulked-up steroid case with a porn star mustache. He gave Max a nasty stare. He gave the gleaming Porsche an even nastier one. The easy rich man/poor man math was all over his face: Just the annual insurance bill on this hot rod added up to more than the officer's take-home pay.

Right now Max was just an anonymous rich brat. The only way to handle police like this was to be obsequious until the famous daddy card played itself out. Until then, he'd keep a wary eye on the trigger-happy finger flirting with the Taser that dangled from the cop's hip. Miami-Dade's finest were no strangers to zapping twelve-year-olds who skipped school with 50,000-volt shocks. A teenage speed demon could easily get that for so much as mouthing off.

"Is there a problem, Officer?" Max asked. It was the best

he could manage in terms of respect for authority, though the impression lingered that the word "officer" should be substituted with "dumb ass." He dutifully handed over his license and registration. Then he started the silent countdown. One thousand one . . . one thousand two . . .

"Hey, are you Max Biaggi's kid?" Cop code for "almost off the hook."

Max smiled yes.

The officer's puffed-up attitude deflated faster than a pricked balloon. Now his posture was that of goobed-out fan. "*Hijack* is one of my all-time favorite movies." Cop code for "*definitely* off the hook."

"Yeah," Max wanted to say, "that's why he got twenty-five million for *Hijack II.* Because of idiots like you." But he just grinned, as if the news made him proud to be his father's son, which, considering what bullshit that was, made Max the better actor in the family.

"Tell you what," the officer began, "I'll let you go with a warning this time." He scribbled an address onto the back of a business card. "And if you could get your dad to send me an autographed picture, that'd be great. Have him inscribe it to Philip. One L. It's on the front."

Max smiled, slipping the card into a storage slot on the dashboard. "Consider it done." Of course, once he took off, he'd toss it out the window and feed it to the wind.

"Let me ask you something," the cop said. His voice went down an octave. "What's he like in real life?"

Max wanted to laugh. If the officer only knew how toxic that question was. His father didn't exactly save the world from terrorist plots, escape machine-gun fire with a drop-and-roll, or protect his family at all costs. No, that was the big-screen Max Biaggi. The "real-life" version was a total lame ass, the kind of man who couldn't do a single sit-up without his personal trainer barking out motivation, the kind of father who treated his kids as nothing more than *People* magazine photo ops.

But Philip the action film fan didn't wait for an answer. His big fist playfully punched Max's shoulder. "I'm probably embarrassing you, huh? I bet you're no different than most kids your age." He laughed a little. "Embarrassed by your parents. Even if your dad is a big star."

"Try 'big asshole,' you brain-dead gym rat." Max had the words ready to play, but he never pressed the button.

"Do me a favor and slow down, okay? I know you want to give this nice ride a road workout. I like to do the same myself sometimes."

"In what, your Ford Taurus?" But again, Max didn't press play.

"Be safe and stay close to those speed limits." He peered at Max a bit more seriously now. "Have you been drinking tonight?"

"No, sir," Max said, the deference turning his stomach as he lied about the Red Bull and Level that he'd hammered down before getting behind the wheel. "I was just in a hurry to pick up a date."

The cop gave him a conspiratorial one-guy-to-another wink. "A kid like you must do pretty good with the girls."

Max pretended to be shy about such things. He just shrugged and allowed himself a half smile. "I do okay." The truth was, in the last two days, he'd hooked up with six different girls. But who kept count?

"Take off, kid. And be careful out there." He started back for his blinking patrol car, then spun around. "And don't forget my autograph!"

But Max Biaggi Jr. was already gone. And the Philip with one L reminder was already flying litter. If that cop wanted an autograph bad enough, he could join the online fan club at maxbiaggi.com for fifty bucks a year and get a machine-signed one.

Max unhooked the Sidekick II from his belt and speed dialed Vanity St. John. Once upon a time, they'd been "friends with benefits." And, oh man, the benefits had been awesome. Now they were just friends, though. Her choice. But Max would go back to the old arrangement anytime. All Vanity had to do was say the word. "What's up, Rope Bitch?" he sang, bobbing his head to the beat and ignoring more traffic signs.

"Turn the music down!" Vanity yelled.

Max faded out Lil Jon and the East Side Boyz. "Is that good?"

"Better," she said. "Where are you?"

"Looking for a party. I just cleaned out Christina and some of her anime freaks. It's time to celebrate."

"Christina's anime crowd?" Vanity's tone was half-incredulous, half-scolding. "God, you must really be desperate."

Max laughed. "Hey, it's all green, baby. It's all green." Word had circulated around Miami that he was the go-to guy for poker—both modest-bet games for the risk-challenged and high-stakes buy-ins for the diehard gamblers.

They usually took place at the famous Max Biaggi mansion on Star Island. Max Jr. and Shoshanna, his fifteen-year-old sister, claimed the basement as a playroom. It was a cool hangout—pool table, a few surfboards, plasma-screen TV, Xbox, and a stereo-enabled iPod. Max preferred being the host. That way he could relax, have fun, keep a running tally of who owed what on his Mac laptop, and shrewdly decide which small-timers might be ready for some bigger action.

As for Christina Perez and her crew? Definitely not. Those pathetic souls had entered his poker sanctum with designs on tripling their weekly allowances to get to some anime convention in Dallas. Granted, Christina had left with some pride. But the others limped out with crushed hearts and flattened wallets. One dude lost his entire Gap paycheck for the last two weeks of mall slavery. Sucker.

Max's game of choice was Texas Hold 'Em. Simple five-card deal. At least it seemed that way. Ha. Players cruising on ego fuel were quick to delude themselves into thinking they were poker aces, and eager virgins were quick to bet big on what they thought would be a sure hand. At the end of the day, it was all about strategy. Winning meant thinking like a chess champion.

Max didn't just love the game. He was officially obsessed. After all, being good at poker was all about lying and deception. Ask any hot girl in the 305 area code about his age: Max could lie and deceive his ass off. A tense game in his basement was the ultimate thrill ride. He could always tell who had a killer pair of cards to lay down, who was bluffing to stay in the mix, and who was heading for a money meltdown.

"Poor Christina," Vanity lamented. "How much did she lose?"

"Don't worry. She ended up holding her own," Max said. "The girl won't be posting her *Sailor Moon* DVDs on eBay next week."

"Right," Vanity said. "She'll just be hawking her art supplies and basically selling off her future." One beat. "All because of you."

Just like Max and Vanity, Christina would be a senior in the fall at the Miami Academy for Creative and Performing Arts. She was crazy for Japanese anime and dreamed of having her own series one day. And Max had no doubt that she would. Christina knew what she wanted and she worked toward it every single day. Meanwhile, Max and Vanity called themselves acting majors, but they were both just coasting through to graduation.

"Where should we meet up?" Max asked. "Black Sand?"

"Maybe Mynt," Vanity said. "Mimi says I should put in an appearance there tonight."

Max shook his head, grinning. Mimi as in Mimi Blair, Vanity's power girl publicist. Not many seventeen-year-old girls had their own handler to tell them where to go and how long to stay there. How wicked cool was that? Shit. Maybe he should get one. And if they all looked as smoking hot as Mimi, why not hire two? His father would sign off on the bill. Action Dad preferred the spending of money to the spending of time anyway.

Yeah, that's what Max needed. His own publicist. He worshiped Donald Trump. Something about the man fascinated Max. For one thing, he was drawn to the way Trump walked around as if he were ten feet tall, no matter what business analysts, critics, or late-night comedians were saying about him. Freaking brilliant. Especially the methods he used to promote his own image. They were awesome. And a man needed some strong PR muscle to brand himself. One night, a few months ago, when Max and Vanity were almost drunk and counting up his winning stash, she'd pronounced him Baby Donald. The name stuck. Now it was even on his license plate in abbreviated form: BABY DON.

"Are you there?" Vanity asked.

Her question rocked him back to the issue of Mynt. It was a South Beach superclub with deep green walls that got washed in menthol green light. Pretty cool. They said that the scent of mint wafted through the air vents, but every time

Max had ever partied there, all he could smell was cigarettes, sweat, and sex. "Yeah, I'm here," he said, finally. "We'll meet you there."

Vanity hesitated. "Who's *we*?"

"Pippa," Max answered. "I'm on my way to pick her up now."

Vanity groaned. "Well, so much for that pot of cash you won tonight. The girl won't have a dollar to her name. Trust me."

"I thought you liked her."

"I do. But she never has any money." Vanity launched into a mocking British accent. "I'm so broke. Please buy me a Vitamin Water. Can you pay for my movie ticket?" Then she sighed heavily. "God, it's so annoying. I've only known her a few weeks, and the girl owes me at least a hundred dollars! I mean, come on, I thought her father was a millionaire."

"He is," Max said. One beat. "Or was. I'm not sure what the deal is. All I know for sure is that her mother divorced him and that they moved here with practically nothing. Did you know she only gets sixty bucks a week for allowance money?" He laughed. "Shit, I spend that much on *gum.*"

"Sixty dollars?" Vanity echoed. The shock in her voice said the amount sounded more like sixty cents. "Well, that explains why she was wearing an Old Navy outfit the other day." Bitchy laugh. "Maybe we should start a relief fund. You know, like they did for the Tsunami victims."

"Oh, baby, you're *cold,*" Max said. But his voice rang with nothing but praise. He loved every second of it. His Sidekick II alerted him to a text message. One glance. "Speak of the devil. I just got a text from her. Hold up." Checking the screen, he read it and smiled.

WHERE THE HELL R U?

Then he quickly typed out a reply.

ON THE WAY. C U SOON.

"Okay, I'm back. She was like, 'Where the hell are you?' I'm telling you, the girl wants me."

"Either that or the free drinks," Vanity countered.

"Be nice," Max warned. "Seriously, Pippa's really nervous about being the new girl in the fall."

"Oh, so you're just there for her on a social level." Vanity's voice dripped with sarcasm.

"Not *entirely*," Max admitted. "The girl *is* hot. I wouldn't mind marking my territory before we go back to school."

"God, you're such a pig!" Vanity laughed.

"Hey, I need to get to her before the new guy does."

"What new guy?" Vanity asked.

"Oh, it's my stepmonster's new charity project," Max said. "She's fronting tuition for our housekeeper's son to join MACPA's music program."

"Let me guess. He wants to be a DJ or a rapper."

"How'd you know?"

"Because those are the hip-hop dreams of every maid's

child," Vanity sneered. "You said *you* had to get to Pippa first. Does that mean he's hot?"

Max laughed. "Hot enough for you? Maybe too hot. I'm no fag, but the dude's got some serious babe mojo. Once, during a party he was supposed to be working, he nailed two catering waitresses in our pool house. The man was my personal hero for a week. I've never scored like that, and I'm freaking Max Biaggi *Jr.*"

"I can't *wait* to meet him," Vanity said with faux sincerity. Clearly, it was the last thing she wanted to do. "I need to go. Mimi just got here. I'll see you at Mynt." And then she was gone.

Max grinned as he slipped the Sidekick II back onto his belt clip. He had a feeling that if any guy could melt the ice princess that was Vanity St. John, then that guy was Dante Medina. Oh, yeah. It promised to be a *very* interesting senior year.

Pippa Keith lived in a rundown Deco-style studio cottage off Miami Beach, and when Max pulled into the cracked concrete drive, she was standing outside, lit by moonbeams, and hotter than he remembered.

Damn. The girl was dressed to assassinate male hormones in a black micromini and tight white tank with SEXPERT spelled out in big naughty letters. He felt a stiffening in his jeans that had nothing to do with new denim. And a flush on his face that had nothing to do with the heat.

Pippa looked like a Britney clone from the "I'm a Slave 4 U" era. She was all long blonde hair, sweat-slicked body, and honey-brown tan. Plus, her English accent rocked, and her funny British way of saying things was cute as hell.

She slid into the passenger seat and slammed the door. "I didn't think you'd ever come 'round the house." Gucci Envy Me cologne perfumed the tiny cabin with hints of peony, jasmine, and pink pepper.

Superman had X-ray vision. Max Biaggi Jr. had sex-ray vision. He gave Pippa Keith a long and hard dose of it, trying to keep his mouth shut. Then he decided to watch the road. Because drooling behind the wheel of a Porsche just wasn't cool.

"I'm so glad you called," Pippa said. "I was bored rigid sitting there with my mum watching a soppy DVD."

He grinned at her turns of phrase. "How'd you sneak out?"

"I told her that I had a dodgy tummy and was going to bed for the night." She waved a hand, dismissing the low-rent life already a few miles behind. "I feel like getting full-on trashed. Will you buy my drinks tonight? I'm low on cash."

Max smiled to himself, hearing Vanity's I-told-you-so voice in his head. He gave Pippa a bold glance. "What's in it for me?"

"What do you mean?"

Max beamed over a look that said he knew that she knew exactly what he meant.

"I'm not snogging you!" Pippa said, a huge grin on her

face as she protested meekly. "I thought we were just mates."

"It's after midnight, and we're on our way to Mynt to get drunk," Max pointed out.

"I'm not snogging you!" Pippa maintained.

Max played with the sound system until Snoop Dogg and Pharrell exploded from the speakers and vibrated his rib cage. "Mynt charges about fourteen bucks a drink," he yelled over the music.

"You better look now!" Pippa screamed. And then she hooked her fingers beneath the micromini and lifted her skirt the few inches that mattered.

Max swallowed hard, his eyes glued onto the triangle of white lace against her slim brown thighs.

"And that's all you're getting!" Pippa announced triumphantly.

"For now," Max told her. And then he played NASCAR driver all the way to Mynt, stoked and ready for some Formula One fun.

From: Dante

I'm on a sky terrace, dawg. The nanny's hot
as shit and needs swim lessons 2. I get paid
for this? LOL.

10:09 am 6/18/05

chapter three

"Call me Lala," Adelaida Famosa intoned seductively. "That's what the children say . . . Nanny Lala."

Dante struggled to maintain his trademark cool. Ordinarily, hot girls were no big deal. Treat them that way and you could have your pick. But Lala was gorgeous to a degree that defied all reason. Salma Hayek could be her *ugly* sister. That's how fine she was.

So this was crazy luck on top of crazy luck. And he owed it all to SafeSplash, an agency that employed instructors to teach at-home swim lessons to rich kids in Miami.

Lala leaned in to clutch Dante's arm as she dipped her pink-polished toes into the cerulean waters of the sky terrace pool. "Ooh!" she squealed, pressing closer as she giggled and expressed alarm about how cold it was.

Dante experienced a stiffening where it counted. Suddenly, he crouched down to test the temperature himself. The truth was, a blast of something cold could only do him good right now.

Any minute, the man who hired him, Simon St. John, megamillionaire, music mogul, rags-to-riches dream maker, could step into view. And catching the new swim coach making a tent out of his trunks on account of the young and nubile nanny was *not* the first impression that Dante wanted to make. Besides, there was no way St. John would have a live-in that looked like this and not be hitting it on a regular basis. Best to stay clear.

Just as Dante began gliding his left hand through the water, he felt the pinch of Lala's nails dig into his back, then a firm shove sent him tumbling into the pool. He went down. He came up. He shook his head to free the chlorine from his eyes.

Lala stood there laughing hysterically, her considerable attributes bouncing up and down, coming close to escaping the bikini halter that barely contained them. But in the end, the tiny string held firm. A minor miracle. And one of God's crueler special effects.

Dante's mind began to drift. Those sensible thoughts from mere moments ago turned to dirty ones. Feeling cocky—and getting no relief from the cold water—he peeled off his drenched Hollister T-shirt and tossed it onto the deck with a loud *plop.* "Now it's your turn." He smiled at her. "Jump in."

Lala giggled, inching away from the edge. "I can't swim."

"That's why I'm here," Dante said. "To teach you."

"Can I hold on to you?"

He grinned. "Absolutely."

"Maybe you should just start by giving her mouth to mouth," a female voice said sharply. "Apparently, that's what she really wants."

Dante spun around to find Vanity St. John standing on the opposite side of the pool, a beach beauty fantasy in her white bikini and sheer sarong.

"I didn't think girls like you got up before the crack of noon," Dante teased.

Even with her eyes eclipsed by huge Chanel sunglasses, Vanity looked anything but amused. She shifted the small stack of celebrity magazines in her hands. "And I didn't think boys like you could find a job that didn't require a polyester uniform and a name tag."

"Burger King was last summer's gig," Dante said matter-of-factly. "This one pays better. And you can't beat the scenery." He purposefully dropped the line with heavy ambiguity. Was he referring to Vanity, Lala, or both of them?

Vanity beamed a disapproving glare across the pool to the Cuban caregiver. "Lala, here's a news flash: The twins' art camp ended about fifteen minutes ago. Do you expect two three-year-olds to just take a cab home?"

Lala murmured some unintelligible Spanish as she went scrambling inside.

Vanity rolled her eyes and made a beeline for an expansive, white terry cloth-covered chaise lounge. She walked with the sprocket-hipped gait of a supermodel navigating the runway of the hottest fashion show on earth—confident, predatory, like a sleek panther juiced up on Red Bull.

Dante found himself mesmerized. So few girls played hard to get with him, and when they did, the instant challenge it conjured up was intoxicating as hell. He swam toward her.

But Vanity didn't just ignore him. She put on a show about it, theatrically refusing to so much as glance in his direction, pretending to be engrossed in the latest *Us Weekly* that featured yet another Lindsay Lohan scandal on the cover.

He hoisted himself out of the pool and stood up—and up, and up, and up to his full height, posture ramrod straight, abdominals rippling, Quicksilver board shorts dripping. "I never saw you in the club last night."

She flicked one page to the next without moving her eyes. "Which one? I hit three or four."

"Black Sand. You let me in. Remember?"

In a pantomime of boredom, she tossed down *Us* and snatched up *In Touch*. "I let in a lot of people. Anyway, I didn't go inside because that club is so over."

"You were at the door," Dante pointed out. "Does that mean you're over, too?"

Vanity gave a little huff before turning on him hotly. But

her annoyance turned to comeuppance as her gaze zeroed in on something over his shoulder. All of a sudden, her lips curled into a grin. "Not as over as you're about to be."

"Hey!" an authoritative male voice bellowed accusingly. "Are you the coach from SafeSplash?"

Dante's heart went *bang* as his mind let loose with a stream of silent, self-reprimanding curses: You stupid, horned-up asshole. You're about to get fired before you even start. Slowly, dreadfully, he turned around. "Yes, sir."

"Did I hire you to teach my kids how to swim or to hit on my daughter?" Simon St. John concentrated hard on his BlackBerry, jabbing at the device with nimble thumbs while waiting for an answer. He stood there in what had to be a custom-tailored suit, dove gray for the season, dressed to deal in megabucks. A pack of storm troopers would be less intimidating.

Dante walked over at a fast clip. "To teach your kids, of course, sir. I'm Dante Medina." He offered his hand.

Simon St. John ignored it. "What's that?" He gestured to the sopping-wet lump that was Dante's T-shirt.

"Oh, that's my shirt, sir. I—"

"Get it out of my sight."

"Yes, sir. I—"

"We signed up for ten thirty-minute lessons. Can you guarantee that my kids will be swimmers by the end?"

"Yes, sir. That's my goal."

"Good. Make sure you achieve it. Now clean up your shit

and leave my daughter alone. Lala will be back with the kids shortly." He started off.

"Excuse me, sir," Dante called after him respectfully. "May I adjust the pool temperature?"

St. John stopped and pierced Dante with a cold glare. "Why do you want to do that?"

"Our experience has been that the most successful teaching at young ages happens in water of about ninety-one degrees."

"I swim in the morning and prefer it cooler," St. John snapped. "Keep it at eighty." And then he was gone.

"Medina, could you be a bigger dumb ass?" he murmured to himself. Talk about a master plan turning to shit in a heartbeat. The whole point of getting this job in the first place had been to create opportunity. Dante had read about young struggling actors in Hollywood who got breaks in the industry thanks to connections made from teaching the children of producers and agents how to swim.

That's why he trained with the senior instructors at Safe-Splash, took a class in CPR, and nearly went psycho when he realized that the three-year-old twins of Simon St. John were on his summer roster. It was the kind of luck so perfect that Dante considered it a sign from above.

Simon St. John was the CEO of Alcatraz Recordings, a company fast rivaling Def Jam as a leader in hip-hop music, style, and culture. At first, there'd been controversy and suspicion. After all, what did a rich white man know about hip-hop? But St. John had an eye for talent and an ear for music, no matter the style. Over the years, the man had taken pop, rock, dance, alternative, country, Latin, and jazz acts to platinum status.

Dante dreamed of making his own music one day. He possessed the rhyme skills, the talent to create killer beats, and the discipline to fill notebooks with lyrics. The truth was, he lived and breathed hip-hop, spending hours analyzing the music of innovators like the Ying Yang Twins, the Game, Eminem, Mike Jones, and Kanye West.

But the key to breaking out was coming up with a new sound. The Houston scene had done it with Screw, a crazy method of slowing records down, chopping them up, and manipulating the beats to repeat favorite words and phrases. Dante felt like he had the edge on a sick new sound that would someday be known as distinctively Miami. All he needed was a believer with the right Rolodex. Someone like Simon St. John.

"Sorry about that," Vanity said, breaking into Dante's private reverie. "My dad's a total dick." She was front and center now, smelling like Coppertone and fully aware of her power to fatally distract.

"Actually, I'm the dick," Dante muttered. He leaned down to pick up his T-shirt, pulling it over his head and onto his body, struggling with the wet cotton.

"Don't worry. He won't remember anything that happened this morning," Vanity assured him. "Half the time he doesn't even realize what he says to people."

Dante regarded her warily. The girl seemed vaguely depressed, and he wondered how this could be. Here she lived in a tropical oasis, on a private oceanfront at the end of South Beach, away from the neon lights and congestion of Ocean Drive. Okay, maybe her father didn't have the charm of a morning talk show host, but at least the man was still around. And as for her future, it was damn sure secure. Anything she wanted to be was just a phone call or family favor away. Meanwhile, he was hustling for a break—any break.

"How old are you?" Vanity asked.

"Seventeen," Dante offered, staring out beyond the terrace and into the infinite ocean.

"Where do you go to school?"

"I'm transferring to MACPA in the fall," he answered distantly.

Vanity's lips parted, and a ripple of awareness seemed to skate across her perfectly symmetrical face.

But Dante was done flirting. The last thing on his mind was tapping *this* particular ass. From now on, Vanity St. John was strictly off-limits. "No offense, but when I took this job, pissing off your father wasn't part of my master plan. I should probably concentrate on my work."

Suddenly, as if responding to a stage cue, Lala emerged from the house, flanked by two energetic little blonds, one boy and one girl, both beaming excited smiles and already suited up for the water. "Gunnar and Mercedes," Lala announced, "this is Dante. He's going to teach us how to swim."

Dante crouched down to address them at eye level. "Are you kids ready to have some fun?"

The twins offered shy nods in answer. Finally, the little boy spoke. "I want to go under the water like a shark!"

"Me, too!" the girl echoed.

Dante laughed. He raised a palm in the high-five gesture. "If you want to learn that, I can teach it."

Gunnar and Mercedes slapped his fingers with their little palms and collapsed into fits of kiddie laughter.

At that moment, Dante made it his personal mission to take them far beyond Simon St. John's expectations. The man might not think much of their coach right now, but when he saw these children swim at the end of ten lessons, it would be a whole new attitude. In fact, Dante planned to make them so fearless in the water that St. John would think what Michael Phelps did in a pool was called drowning. "Ready to get started?"

Gunnar and Mercedes jumped up and down and screamed in response.

Dante grinned, rising up to stand between the children, taking two tiny hands in his and playfully marching forward. His gaze scanned the area for Vanity.

But she was gone.

Vanity *knew*, with all the certainty she felt that Mary-Kate Olsen just needed to get over her food issues and eat a bagel, that Dante Medina was the housekeeper's son that Max had been talking about last night.

Please. It *had* to be him. What were the odds? How many working-class boys could be transferring to MACPA in the fall?

And the only reason pissing off her father wasn't part of his "master plan" was because the hip-hop wannabe hoped he could get an inside edge on a recording deal. Ooh, how cunning. If the poor guy only knew. Teaching toddlers how to float would hardly put him on the fast track with Simon St. John.

On the way to lock herself into her bedroom and shut out the world, Vanity snatched a bottle of Voss water from the Sub-Zero fridge. After telling *Elle Girl* in a miniquestionnaire that it was her favorite H²O, the company had started sending her cases by the truckload.

She fired up the Green Day CD in her Bang & Olufsen BeoSound One. "Boulevard of Broken Dreams" began to blast. She flung her body onto the unmade bed and fired up the Apple iBook to check e-mail. While the system uploaded, she rolled onto her back and stared up at the ceiling.

She hated her asshole father.

She hated that stupid slut Lala.

She hated those annoying twins.

Oh, God, was she a monster bitch for hating innocent children? It's just that every time she looked at Gunnar and Mercedes, Vanity experienced a feeling of envy so powerful that she feared it might turn toxic. Like her, they were motherless. The twins had been born out of wedlock to her father's former assistant, Blythe Barnhill, a flake who quickly signed away her parental rights and left Miami to tour the country with the bass player in a punk metal band called Blood and Guts.

So the empathy should be there, right? After all, her own mother, Isis St. John, had been absent from the scene for more years than Vanity wanted to remember. The ex-cover girl was in and out of rehab centers for alcohol, drugs, and eating disorders, not to mention a tabloid favorite for crashing and burning one dead-end relationship after another—the aging rock star, the volatile actor, the lesbian restauranteur. Once a supermodel, always a headline.

Still, Vanity felt no tenderness toward the twins for their shared maternal void. Maybe it was because her father looked after them with a devotion that he'd never shown his first and oldest child. It's like Vanity woke up one morning and all the unfairness of the world had been staring her in the face. How could she walk around and pretend that everything was okay?

Sometimes all she wanted to do was steal away into the dark and carve "hypocrite" into her arm with a razor. Her father was one. But then again, she was, too. There existed a public image of Vanity St. John—fashionista, hot-bodied trendsetter, guy magnet, supremely confident smart-ass.

And then, late at night, where Vanity really lived, there

existed the truer version of herself. She was lonely. Everything felt like such a struggle. A sense of worthlessness often consumed her. This notion that girls all over the country—the world even—yearned to trade places with her seemed absurd. In all honesty, Vanity would gladly swap lives with, say, an overweight girl from South Dakota, someone with two parents who were her biggest fans, someone with friends who didn't want anything from her, someone who woke up in the morning with a sense of joy and didn't spend the rest of the day wondering, "Who am I supposed to be?"

The iBook was up and ready. Vanity signed onto AOL, listened to the familiar "You've got mail!" announcement crackle through the speakers, and scrolled through the new postings. There was one from Dr. Parker confirming her next appointment. Which reminded her. The refill on her pills had expired, and she was almost out. Mimi had sent a note with an attachment. Probably a schedule of every place she was supposed to show up this week. Vanity didn't open it. She just forwarded it straight to her Sidekick II. Why hadn't Mimi sent the message there in the first place? Stupid bitch.

Suddenly, an instant message invaded the screen.

britgirl88: hey! what r u doing?

Ugh. It was Pippa. So the girl was still breathing after last night's vodka bender that gave her the courage to dance on top of the bar at Mynt while every perv in the club (Max included) stared up her skirt and took bets on whether she had a Brazilian wax or just a neatly trimmed bush. Of course, Max cleaned them out.

Vanity groaned and began to type.

vanity6: just hanging out.

britgirl88: i'm SO bored! max is playing poker all day. wanna go shopping??

vanity6: maybe later.

britgirl88: i have NO money. big shock! but i dug up a few receipts so i can take some shit back and start over. brilliant!!

vanity6: yes, u r quite the rocket scientist.

britgirl88: lol

Vanity's T-Mobile device blasted to life to the ringtone of Gwen Stefani's "Hollaback Girl." She zapped the remote control to silence Green Day and hit the speakerphone feature, not recognizing the incoming number. "Hello?"

"Hey, hot girl. You looked good last night." It was Jayson "J.J." James. "I had my eye out for you inside. What happened?"

"It was too B-list, so I left," Vanity said.

Pippa launched another IM.

britgirl88: what time do u wanna go?

"Yeah, my brother was in town and wanted to check it out,"

J.J. explained. "I wanted to hit Mynt, but he swore up and down that he read it'd gone gay." He laughed a little. "I got sick of arguing with his dumb ass."

Vanity said nothing.

"You there?" J.J. asked.

"Yeah, I'm here."

Pippa was getting anxious.

britgirl88: u still there??

"We should hook up later," J.J. suggested. "I'm on my way to the gym, but I'll be finished in a few hours. There's a kick-ass party at the Surfcomber tonight."

Vanity felt the sensation of brain fireworks. Thoughts of her father, Lala, the twins . . . and Dante . . . exploded in her mind. Right now the impulse to get away from them made even J.J. seem appealing. "I'm in. Call me later." She hung up.

Pippa was officially freaking out.

britgirl88: hello???

Vanity left her to wonder and signed off AOL without answering. Then she rang her publicist to get the lowdown.

"Mimi Blair."

"Hey, it's Vanity. What's going on at the Surfcomber tonight?"

"A party for Fresh Faces in Fashion," Mimi answered automatically. "It's on your schedule for a Hitchcock. No more than ten minutes. Show up, snap a few pictures, get the hell out. The buzz event is a CD launch party at the Ritz-Carlton for Katee K."

Vanity made a face. Katee K was the latest Disney Channel sitcom star to poison the airwaves with pop music so bad it could kill on first listen.

"I know," Mimi said, as if reading Vanity's mind. "The little bitch sucks, but her song's in the top five, she just signed a development deal with Paramount, and *everybody* wants into this party . . . that's the wrong color . . . take it off . . . *take it off* . . . sorry, I'm trying to get a pedicure, and this woman doesn't speak a word of English."

"I'll let you go," Vanity laughed, her mind already on other things, mainly forecasting the night ahead. No doubt J.J. would have a room booked at the Surfcomber and invent some lame excuse to lure her up there. No doubt she would go willingly and be down for whatever.

It's not like she was unaware of the male model's game. She knew J.J. was a player and probably just using her for sex and a good photo op. And deep down, Vanity didn't know if she was even worth more than that.

She rolled over and started to cry, eventually falling to sleep.

From: Mom

I'm off to a late meeting. Won't be home for
dinner. Eat something healthy. No junk food!
Love, M

6:13 pm 6/19/05

chapter four

It was 1997, and Daisy Fuentes was hosting MTV's *House of Style.* That's when Christina Perez knew she was gay. The beautiful, Havana-born starlet made her feel funny, and Christina thought about her when she went to bed.

But now, years later, on nights like this, she thought about someone else—a real girl, not a television fantasy. Of course, at the end of the day, this crush was no different. It was *still* a fantasy. Christina would never get the chance to fulfill her secret desires—to touch the girl, to kiss her, to smell her. She knew this because ever since she could remember, the dreams she wished for the most never came true.

That's why she found a private sanctuary in *shojo manga,* the Japanese comics that were romantic, full of angst and emotion, and all about love. Some of her favorites were *Fruits Basket, Alice 19th,* and, especially *Marmalade Boy.* That title, about a high school girl who instantly falls for her new step-brother, was a great example of what anime fans called a "love dodecahedron," code for a simple love triangle gone insanely complex with the introduction of additional characters and more crushes.

Sometimes Christina felt like Yuu Matsuura, the title character of *Marmalade Boy.* Like him, she had both a bitter side and a sweet side. But most people overlooked this and just regarded her as a kook. After all, she liked comics (even if they were cool *manga* books, they were still mere comics to her peers), and she dismissed Miami's skin-baring fashion trends in favor of Dumpster chic.

Christina was bone-thin and generally cold-natured, so it was easy for her to wear chadorlike layers in the summer and not be too warm. Her one big extravagance was a pair of enormous Laura Biagiotti sunglasses that practically eclipsed her whole face. Everything else in her closet was comprised of thrift shop, garage sale, and consignment store finds.

Tonight she was clad in ripped jeans, over which she threw on a chiffon miniskirt with unfinished hem. Add her scuffed boots and the two moth-eaten cashmere sweaters she layered on top, and you had, in the immortal words of her mother, political barracuda Paulina Perez, "an unmade bed" or "a bag lady," the latter indicating her only parent's highest level of disapproval.

Was she really her mother's daughter? Christina had to stop and wonder. Paulina Perez was a card-carrying friend of the radical right. She voted Republican. She fought for moral values. She was even being groomed for national office. The unofficial word was that the party would put money and muscle behind her to run for a retiring senator's Florida seat.

The mere thought filled Christina with a chilling dread. Even now, without the pressure of an election bearing down, her mother was impossible.

I wish you wouldn't walk around looking like a homeless girl. People will think I can't afford to dress my own daughter . . .

Do you want to know why you never have any dates? Boys probably think you're weird because you never put down those stupid comic books . . .

I gave in on the argument to send you to MACPA, but I'm not wasting your college savings on art school. You're going to get a real education . . .

Oh, God, she could actually hear Paulina's nagging voice right now. In fact, it was ringing inside Christina's head in that carefully enunciated, modulated tone that betrayed no hint of Hispanic roots. This from a woman whose own mother spoke little to no English. The truth was, Paulina was on a mission to leave her past behind, to join the ranks of the haves and forget the have-nots.

Sure, Christina's mother would play up the poor immigrant act on the campaign trail. It made for good media when she wrapped the flag around it and called herself the living embodiment of the American dream. But none of her platform issues had anything to do with the struggling poor. No way. Her mother's one-trick pony was the moral values crusade. Why? Because it earned her the most TV coverage and generated attention from the national party.

At home, Paulina would go off on extended rants, practicing for stump speeches and impromptu microphone moments. Christina just tuned her out, either jacking up the volume on her iPod or getting lost in a *manga*. She could never figure out why the so-called moral issues that generated the most attention were always the same. If it wasn't two men wanting to get married, then it was a stupid video game that somebody deemed too violent. Meanwhile, people were starving, losing jobs along with their retirement savings, and going without health care because they didn't have any insurance. But hey, let's stop the two boys from planning a wedding. Whatever.

Suddenly, Christina's Sidekick II jingled to the ringtone of Hi Hi Puffy Ami Yumi's *Teen Titans* theme. She smiled as a digipic of a very happy and very drunk Max Biaggi Jr. flashed on the screen. The reigning king of cool at the Miami Academy for Creative and Performing Arts. It was only recently that he'd begun engaging her as a friend and seeking her out as a social companion. It made Christina feel special and just a little bit cool herself by the association alone. "Hello?"

"What's up, JAP?"

She rolled her eyes with amusement. He loved to tease

her, calling her a Japanese American Princess on account of her *manga* obsession. "Not much. I'm just sitting here trying to decide what to have for dinner."

"You actually *eat?*" Max asked, his tone jokingly incredulous. "All the bitches I know just throw up."

Christina laughed.

"I'm hungry, too. Let's grab a bite."

"Okay," Christina agreed, thrilled at the prospect. Granted, *manga* was her great escape, but sometimes she craved the company of people her own age, too.

"I'm putting together a game for later on," Max went on. "Are you in?"

She hesitated.

"Come on. You're a natural. Besides, this one's just for fun. No major buy-in. A new buddy of mine is coming. You might think he's hot and want to hook up."

"I doubt it."

"What's wrong?" Max taunted her. "Saving yourself for an Asian boy? Maybe a Chinese acrobat will join the school in the fall. You know, somebody like that dude in *Ocean's Eleven.*"

Christina's insides were rocked by the immediate grip of anxiety. At times like this, she longed to tell—somebody, anybody—her secret. But deep down, she knew that Max was hardly the go-to guy for sensitive, heart-on-the-sleeve confessions. After dismissing her inner torment with a vague, "Hey, that's hot," he would probably blow past the serious nature of the announcement and make some boneheaded request like, "Can I watch you make out with another girl?"

"How does sushi sound?" Max asked. "We could go to Maiko. It's pretty cheap. Pippa will probably come along, and I don't see the point in feeding her a five-star meal if she's not giving me any." He laughed. "Or even if she was."

Christina shook her head. Max was *such* a guy.

She waited at Maiko on Washington Avenue. And waited. And waited.

A familiar storm of insecure feelings began to stir. The most humiliating scenarios played tricks with Christina's mind. She imagined Max messing with her, setting her up to hang out at this restaurant like some idiot while he and Pippa went to another place and laughed about it.

Christina felt anger bubble up as her worst fears kicked in, working overtime, reliving old middle school memories of isolation and torment—for being different, for dressing in her own style, for retreating into her own world to avoid the painful awkwardness. She ran through Max's possible betrayal from A to Z, including what she would say the next time that she saw him. It would *not* be pretty.

All of a sudden, Max crashed through the door, laughing and pulling a barely dressed Pippa behind him.

Christina's pissed-off mood faded so fast that she felt like a fool for getting worked up in the first place. Instantly, all was forgiven. She glanced around at the surrounding tables, some filled with clubbers loading up on soba noodle soup as stomach prep for a night ahead of heavy drinking, others graced with model types nibbling on Maiko's famous steamed dumplings with *ponzu* sauce. Now that her table would also be occupied beyond a party of one, Christina beamed with pride. Finally, the furtive glances at the pathetic girl eating alone could stop.

Max slid into the seat opposite Christina, snapped his fingers for the waitress, and demanded several orders of kissing rolls the moment she stepped over.

Pippa plopped down next to him, her nipples jutting out like baby bullets in an impossibly snug baby tee emblazoned with LAST NIGHT MEANT NOTHING across the chest. She giggled. "What's a kissing roll?"

"Crab, avocado, cucumber, and little flying-fish eggs," Max informed her.

Pippa pulled a face. "Ew!"

Christina smiled. "It's better not to know what's in the sushi rolls. Just dip them in soy sauce and move on. That's what I do."

Pippa's Marc Jacobs bag began to ring. She pulled out an older model Motorola, the kind with no QWERTY keyboard for easy text-messaging.

Max glanced at the ancient device and gave it a derisive snicker. "Answer the phone, Quaker girl."

Pippa scowled at the screen, rolling her eyes. "It's my bloody mum." She shoved it back into her purse.

Christina tried not to think of her own mother and how furious she would be once she arrived home to find the vague "out with friends" note on the refrigerator. Any moment now Christina's Sidekick II would start blowing up.

Max shook his head and took in the restaurant with a circular gaze, stopping to zero in on a booth packed tight with older guys and younger girls. His jaw clenched with tension at the sight. "Shoshanna!" he called out gruffly.

Christina watched a gorgeous brunette reluctantly extricate herself from the group and stomp over with no shortage of dramatics, her nubile body on display in dangerously low-waisted white denim jeans, so tight as to be painted on. The cleavage spilling out of her top—a lilac camisole by Miguelina—was a special effect worthy of anything George Lucas could dream up at Industrial Light and Magic.

"Does Dad know you're here?" Max grilled her without preamble.

Shoshanna huffed. "Does Dad give a shit?"

It was a rhetorical question. And clearly one Max knew the correct answer to, because he quickly moved on. "How old are those guys you're with?"

"Old enough to rent a limousine and buy us drinks and food all night." Shoshanna pursed her wet, glossy lips, then rolled her eyes. "Like you didn't party when you were my age."

Christina stole a glance at the men in question. They were obviously postcollege age, under thirty but pushing it to fit in that category. Then she found her gaze returning to Shoshanna's breasts.

That's when Max's not-so-baby sister shot her a dirty look. "No, they're not real," she snapped.

Christina felt an instant pink rise high on her cheeks.

Pippa cackled.

Max shook his head again. "My dad bought her implants for her fifteenth birthday. How screwed-up is that?"

Very, Christina wanted to answer, but she just sat there silently.

"Screwed-up would be a botched job," Shoshanna said, cupping her hands under the plastic surgery handiwork to showcase them further. "These are perfect." A quick look at Christina. "I told him that I wanted Jessica Simpson's boobs, and that's exactly what I got."

"Those are nice milkers, not mosquito bites like hers," Pippa put in, pointing at Christina's chest, which, by comparison, was so flat that she felt like a little boy.

Shoshanna burst into laughter, followed by Pippa, and, after losing a short battle to fight it off, Max, too.

Christina was mortified. Still, she smiled gamely in an effort to be a good sport.

The waitress returned with the kissing rolls, and Shoshanna snatched a piece before they hit the table, stuffing it into her mouth with a triumphant grin.

"Hey," Max protested lightly. "I thought your perverted uncles over there were feeding you tonight."

Shoshanna rolled her eyes. "They like the beef teriyaki. Guys in finance can be so lame."

"So ditch those losers and eat with us," Max suggested.

"They rented a stretch Hummer for the night. No way I'm missing that," Shoshanna said. And then she strutted back to her booth.

Christina reached out for a sushi roll, and just as she claimed possession of it, her cellular blasted to life. Exactly as she predicted. Her mother was tracking her down. But unlike Pippa, she couldn't simply ignore the call. Pulling that kind of stunt would risk a missing persons report and a police search. "Hi, Mom."

"Where the hell are you?" Paulina raged.

"I'm at a restaurant with some friends," Christina said innocently. "I left a note on—"

"You don't just go out at night without talking to me first," Paulina cut in angrily. "Get your ass home right now."

"But we're just about to eat," Christina pleaded.

"I don't care," Paulina snapped. "If you don't come home this instant, you'll lose car privileges for the rest of the month." *Click.*

Christina felt the fire of humiliation burn once again—first the crack about her flat chest, now the party-killing intervention of her overprotective mother. Wow. Awesome night out. "I have to go," she grumbled miserably.

Max pulled a face. "Shit, JAP, we were just getting things started."

"I know, but my mom is already threatening terrible things, so . . ."

"You shouldn't have picked up," Max told her.

"I can't believe she's making you go home," Pippa put in. "What a bitch!"

Christina didn't appreciate the fact that Pippa could so casually call her mother a bitch, especially since she'd never met her.

"Call her back and let me talk to her," Max said. "I'm good with parents." He grinned. "Parents love me."

Pippa gave him a strange look. "You're all about a quick shag. Why would parents love you?"

Max hesitated, his lips curled in amusement. "They don't *stay* in love with me. They love me *before* the hit and run." Suddenly, Max grabbed Christina's Sidekick and proceeded to redial the number to the last incoming call.

Christina reached out to snatch it back, but Max twisted beyond her reach, beaming a mischievous smile.

"Yes, Mrs. Perez, this is Max Biaggi Jr. I'm a friend of Christina's. How are you tonight?"

Pippa giggled.

Christina buried her face in her hands. This would only make things worse. She just *knew* it.

"I've been keeping up with your precampaign activities," Max went on. "You know, my father would really appreciate your stand on the issues. A lot of people don't know this, but he's very conservative . . . oh, yes, very much so . . . he only stays closeted to keep those Hollywood liberals happy . . . I'll nudge him to consider a contribution . . . no, I'm happy to do it . . . of course, the real reason for my call is to convince you to let Christina stay with us at least through dinner . . . okay, I'll tell her." Suddenly, he returned the phone, an odd expression on his face.

Christina put it back in her purse. "What did she say?"

"To stop blowing smoke up her ass and to tell you to drive carefully," Max said.

Pippa howled. "That's one mum who *didn't* love you at the first hello."

"Oh, well," Max said easily. "More kissing rolls for us, I guess." And then, using his chopsticks, he proceeded to feed Pippa sushi.

Christina rose up to leave.

"This sucks!" Pippa announced, her mouth full. "Why won't she let you stay?"

Max gave Christina a pained look. "I tried, JAP. But your mom's tough. I'll crack her, though. Just wait. Next time I'll bring my A game, and she won't know what hit her."

Christina waved good-bye as Max and Pippa continued feeding each other. And she wasn't even out of the restaurant when her Sidekick jangled again. Of course, it was her mother. Who else? Sighing heavily, Christina picked up. "I'm leaving, Mom. I'm walking out the door as we speak."

"Drive carefully," Paulina said. "I wanted to tell you that myself. Love you."

"Me, too," Christina whispered. And then she signed off, feeling her spirits sink to an epic low as she realized how happier she would be right now if Max had never called tonight, if she'd just stayed at home and read *Marmalade Boy.*

From: Max

Hey, bitch, where the hell r u? I've left 3
msgs!!!

12:07 am 6/20/05

chapter five

Vanity was practically stoned, yet the fatty had never so much as touched her lips. That's how strong the weed was.

J.J. took another hit and stretched out on the bed. He was shirtless, his cargo shorts were hanging off his narrow hip bones, and he didn't seem to have a care in the world. A total anxiety-free high.

"This is the best shit I've ever smoked," J.J. raved. "It's a strain from the Northeast. They call it Strawberry Cough. Man, it's freaking awesome. Sure you don't want a hit?"

Vanity shook her head. Once upon a time, she'd tried marijuana, and the stuff had made her paranoid as hell. Forget street drugs. She was a liquor and pills girl.

So here they were at the Surfcomber. In a *regular* room

with two double beds. J.J. didn't have enough pull to get up-graded to a suite. Or maybe he just didn't care. Spending five hundred dollars an ounce on reefer was probably more impor-tant than anything else.

The night had been uneventful. As Mimi predicted, the Fresh Faces in Fashion event deserved no more than a ten-minute drive-by, but J.J. had talked Vanity into staying for much longer. Oh, God, Mimi would be so pissed off.

But after enough tequila shots, Vanity didn't care. Screw Katee K's CD launch party. Why should Vanity go out of her way to show up for that little Disney bitch? And screw Pippa. As if Vanity's idea of shopping was watching the British moocher return clothes she'd already worn. That was just gross. Screw Max, too. The only thing he cared about was his stupid poker games. Like Vanity wanted to sit around playing cards all night.

"Jesus Christ, I can't believe how gorgeous you are," J.J. mumbled, pulling her toward him with a lazy arm.

She fell into his embrace, accepting his open-mouth kiss, tentatively at first, then all the way. A fresh strawberry flavor from the premium weed clung to his lips and tongue. Vanity found it exquisitely sweet.

"I could make out with you for hours," J.J. whispered. "You smell so good . . . you taste so good."

The kiss went on and on, never getting too hot as they lulled themselves into a delicious rhythm. It was warm, wet, and wonderful, and so relaxing that Vanity didn't even flinch when J.J.'s slow-moving fingers unfastened the buttons of her People's Liberation denim and scooted down the jeans to expose her thong underwear.

As his hands cupped her ass, his mouth feasted on hers with decidedly more aggression. Suddenly, Vanity felt the sting of a playful slap on her right butt cheek. Shocked, she glanced up at him.

J.J.'s eyes were gleaming naughtily despite their glazed-over look. "Who's your daddy?" he asked thickly. But before she could answer, he popped the left side, too.

For some unknown reason, Vanity started to laugh. Maybe it was the tequila damage, the secondhand high of the Strawberry Cough, or her determination to forget—at least for tonight—that Dante Medina even existed at all. So what if J.J. was a stoner model with limited posing prospects. He was hot, he was too dumb to be anything but straight, and he knew how to make a girl's body tingle. By that measure, he was Orlando Bloom right now.

"Strip for me," J.J. demanded brattily, cradling his hands behind his head and kicking back as if ready to enjoy a show. "Come on. Stand right there and strip for me."

With her jeans already halfway down, Vanity rose up awkwardly. She giggled. "I'm almost naked as it is."

"You need music?" J.J. asked. "I'll give you music." And then he turned into a human beat box and proceeded to serenade her with his woefully bad version of 50 Cent's "Just a Lil Bit."

Instantly, Vanity started to laugh again.

"I wanna unbutton your pants/Just a lil bit/Take 'em off and pull 'em down/A lil bit/Get to kissin' and touchin'/A lil bit . . ."

"*Please* stop. There's nothing worse than a white boy from Iowa trying to rap," Vanity managed to say.

"Come on, baby. Don't be a tease. Strip for me," J.J. said.

Defiantly, Vanity stepped out of her jeans and just stood there, revealing nothing more. "Why don't *you* strip for *me?*"

Without a moment's hesitation, J.J. unsnapped his cargo shorts, pulled them off, and flung them across the tiny room, giving her a full-frontal show in all of his aroused glory. "Done. Your turn."

The stakes were rising.

Vanity slipped off her Dolce & Gabbana lace camisole, let it slink to the floor, and peeled off the nude-colored dimmers that covered her nipples and allowed her to go braless in skimpy tops.

J.J.'s eyes burned up and down her body like heat-seeking lasers. "Turn around."

After a deep breath, she obeyed. It was strange—this notion of her own sexuality, the way it could make her feel so demoralized and empowered at the same time. Guys wanted her. And she could usually make them do almost anything to get her. But rarely were those things what she really needed from them.

"Stand right there . . . and take off your thong," J.J. ordered.

The question hit her now, like it always did at these crucial moments, when she was on the precipice of giving it up to someone undeserving: Who am I supposed to be?

And once again, Vanity didn't have the answer. Here, in this hotel room, at this after-midnight hour, with this selfish, horny guy, she was drawing a complete blank. Well, thank God for that. This set of circumstances was hardly the best scenario in which to address the sixty-thousand-dollar question anyway.

Slowly, she peeled off her underwear. Part of her wanted to flee, but, as was always the case with girls who partied too much, there was enough tequila and secondhand pot smoke in her system to stick around. What the hell? Even though Vanity felt miserable, she knew that she could at least make J.J. happy tonight. And, given the chance, shouldn't somebody in this room be?

Dante laughed so hard that his body convulsed as he scooped the winnings over to his side of the poker table. Was it the two hundred bucks he'd just scored from Hollywood kid Max Biaggi Jr. that he found so damn funny? Or was it the steady stream of Bikini Wax drinks going down faster than Gatorade after a punishing workout? Shit, he was close to wasted. And fast on his way to total oblivion.

Well, if Max thought serving up the one-part vanilla vodka, one-part coconut rum, and one-part pineapple juice concoctions would impact Dante's concentration on the cards, then he definitely knew better by now. It seemed like the more drunk Dante got, the better he played.

A less-disciplined guy would instantly take that logic and start down the road to becoming a gambling alcoholic. But Dante Medina had the discipline of a marine. How else could you explain the fact that he actually stopped himself from hooking up with Vanity St. John? That required the willpower of a monk.

"How'd you do that?" Max demanded. There was a hint of accusation in his tone. His bleary eyes were practically slits.

Pippa sat there waiting for the answer, too, her eyes occasionally rolling to the back of her head. The girl was hammered beyond belief. For every one Bikini Wax that had Dante blitzed, Pippa had probably chased down two.

Dante just laughed at Max. The guy was a sore loser and a bad sport. "Get over it, man. So I cleaned you out. Big deal. I'm sure Daddy will pay off your credit card if you need a cash advance."

The more Max drank, the more pissed off he seemed to get. And he was drinking *a lot.* "For a dude who just learned this game tonight, you caught on pretty fast."

Dante matched Max glare for glare. "What can I say, man? Beginner's luck."

"Luck, my ass," Max said hotly.

"Sheer talent then," Dante countered. And then he pocketed the cash and pushed his chair away from the table.

"Make sure you take that money home to your mother,"

Max snarled. "Who knows? She might take a pay cut this week."

Dante reacted on pure protective instinct. He lunged across the table, grabbed Max's shirt with both hands, and pulled the rich brat toward him until that smart-ass mouth was mere millimeters from his own.

"Get the hell off me, man!" Max cried, trying violently to twist away. But Dante's grip was too strong.

"Cut my mother's salary, and you'll go to the plastic surgeon just like your baby sister. Only it won't be for new tits. It'll be for a new face." And then Dante shook Max loose and watched him fall back into his chair. "Punk ass."

Pippa giggled. "Boys . . . boys . . . boys," she mock scolded, slurring her words. "Just whip them out, and I'll decide which one's bigger." And then she started to laugh uncontrollably at her own joke, so much so that she lost her balance and fell onto the floor.

Nobody bothered to help her get up. The girl was gone. Passed out. Completely shit-faced.

Max's cheeks were burning fire engine red. Too much alcohol and too much humiliation could do that to a guy. "What's your problem, man? Can't you take a joke?"

"Not about my mother," Dante shot back. "That kind of shit will get your ass kicked."

Max glared at him, as if assessing Dante physically and trying to determine what kind of match-up it would be if this came down to an actual fight. The answer seemed to make him laugh. In fact, he cackled so hard that he doubled over. "You could *so* kick my ass, man. It's not even funny."

Feeling his rage subside, Dante looked at Max like he was insane. "Then why are you laughing?"

"Because . . . it's freaking . . . *hilarious,*" Max managed to sputter out as he struggled to his feet, stumbled over, and hooked an arm over Dante's shoulder. "Hey," he whispered confidentially, "sometimes I'm a shit dick when I drink." He put an unsteady finger to his lips. "Don't tell anybody, okay?"

Dante grinned. "You're gone, man." He raised three fingers. "How many am I holding up?"

Max made a show out of zeroing in on Dante's hand. "Uh, I don't know . . . two hundred." And he collapsed into a fit of laughter again.

Dante propped him up to keep his head from hitting the edge of the table.

"I didn't mean that crap about your mom," Max mumbled. "I didn't. Really. I swear." He tried to stand up straight on his own. "Your mom's cool. You're lucky. My mom's a whore. Did you know that?"

Dante winced. From angry drunk to sad, confessional drunk. This would definitely be a long night.

"She let my father pay her off," Max said, blasting a warm breeze of Bikini Wax breath into Dante's face. "Now she lives in New York. New husband. New baby. New family." He brought his voice down to a whisper. "But me and Sho don't fit into the equation. We're part of the old life. The one she wants to forget." Then he waved his hand through the air. The movement caused him to stumble. "Anyway, who cares? She's a whore!"

Even in Max's drunken state, Dante could see the pain transmuted across his face. "We should get you some coffee or water, man. Maybe something to eat, too."

Max shook his head. He went straight to the empty liquor bottles, knocked them down, and drained the shaker for the last remains of the Bikini Wax binge. All of a sudden, he stared down at Pippa and started to laugh. "What should we do with her?"

Dante glanced at the zonked-out girl. "Get her into a bed and let her sleep it off, I guess."

"She's hot," Max observed.

Dante nodded his agreement.

"Think she'd take us both on?" Max said.

Dante looked at him. "Don't know. Don't care. If I want a third party in my action, it's going to be another girl."

"Same here," Max said. "That was just a test. You know, to make sure you're not a fag." And then he fell into another fit of laughter.

Dante found himself unable to resist joining in. "You're sick, man. You really are. You're sick."

"Help me get this drunk bitch onto the sofa," Max said, clumsily walking over to the unconscious girl.

Dante stepped in to assist. Together, he and Max managed to transfer Pippa to the leather sofa and cover her with a blanket. But the effort drained them of what little energy they had left. Almost in perfect unison, they sank down, shoulder to shoulder, propping themselves up against the base of the furniture.

Pippa stirred slightly, and her arm fell down like dead weight onto Max's shoulder.

Dante laughed.

Max just sat there staring into space. "Get a load of this shit, man. I picked this girl up. I bought her dinner. I got her drunk. But I didn't get any. I feel sorry for those dudes in London. What do you think they have to do to get a little head over there?"

Dante shook his head, still laughing. "You're crazy."

"I'm serious, man," Max went on. "I need to find out."

There was a long stretch of silence.

Finally, Dante broke it. "I can't drive," he announced.

"For real?" Max inquired.

"I can't even stand up," Dante said.

"Me, either," Max admitted. "You can crash here."

"I'm cold," Dante said.

Max gave a half-assed look around the basement. "Pippa's got the only blanket."

Dante's eyes fluttered. But he wanted to mess with Max just a little before he gave in to sleep. "Maybe if you hold me, the body heat will get me warm."

"See . . . you are a fag," Max murmured. His head lobbed over to rest heavily on Dante's shoulder. "I knew it." After that, the guy was out cold.

Dante tilted his head against the cushion. And then everything faded into black.

From: Max

U give gr8 head when u r drunk.

7:27 pm 6/21/05

chapter six

Sophie Keith exploded into Pippa's room with no warning knock. "Who is Max?" She wasn't asking the question so much as demanding the answer.

Pippa rolled over to give her intruding mum an evil glare. "Don't you ever knock? God! You're such a commoner sometimes."

"I want to know who this Max person is," Sophie said in a low, seething voice. "I also want to speak to his parents."

Against all argument from her listless, still hungover body, Pippa rose up to get a better beat on the situation. What she noticed next nearly stopped her heart cold.

Nestled in the palm of Sophie Keith's right hand was Pippa's mobile phone.

"You read a text!" Pippa accused hotly. She didn't care

what the message said. It was a *total* invasion of privacy. Somehow she called up the strength to leap from the bed, cross the room, and snatch the device from her nosy mum's manicured paw. It helped that she was furious. This gave her loads of sudden energy. Once in possession of *her* property, she diddled with the tiny keypad to see what had the bitter divorcee channeling Inspector Jane Tennyson or some such telly detective.

U give gr8 head when u r drunk.

Pippa scanned the text but betrayed nothing. She didn't have to. Max was just having a laugh on account of the fact that she got totally trashed and passed out. She flashed an icy look over to her mum. "We're just mates. I haven't even snogged him. It's a joke. That's all."

"I don't think it's very funny," Sophie said primly. "It's disrespectful to write filth like that to a girl."

"Who cares? You're *not* the intended audience," Pippa countered.

Sophie zeroed in with a full-on stare. "You look awful. Were you drinking last night?"

"I didn't booze up. I just had one or two. *Please.* I'm about to start senior school. I'm *not* a child. When are you going to realize that I'm a woman?"

"Is that why you didn't answer my call last night? Because 'as a woman' you were too drunk to have a conversation?"

"Bollocks! Max came 'round the house after you went to

bed. I didn't even have my phone with me. I forgot it," Pippa lied. She proceeded to ignore her interrogator while typing out a reply to the troublemaking text.

Don't remember that at all. U must have a tiny wanger.

Hoorah! Take that, cheeky lad.

"As far as I'm concerned, going somewhere after I've gone to bed is sneaking out of the house," Sophie said.

"Not when you go hiding under the duvet at seven o'clock," Pippa argued. "What am I supposed to do? Watch old *Hollyoaks* tapes till I'm in a coma? You should be happy that I found a few mates that I get on great with."

Wearily, Sophie leaned against the door frame. Her eyes were puffy. No doubt from another crying jag. "I'd still like to meet this Max person before you see him again."

Pippa rolled her eyes. "Whatever. He's a junior. Max Biaggi's firstborn, if you must know."

Sophie's brow lifted in surprise. "The movie star?"

Pippa nodded. "And he's got a bod like Becks and a face like Brad's. Reminds me of that footie captain I went mad for last summer. But don't worry. He's just a boy bud. I won't go rushing in."

"Again, I look forward to meeting him," Sophie said firmly.

"*Fine,*" Pippa relented, crawling back into bed as she wished her moaning mum would bugger off.

But Sophie Keith continued to linger.

Pippa wrestled with the pillows until she got comfortable. Then she stared up at the ceiling and announced, "Here's something to really stress about—I need a cash solution. Everything costs the Earth here. I can't sort out a life on sixty a week. I feel like an old blue rinser who's watching her pension."

Sophie sighed. Almost defeated. But there was a speck of hope. "I'm doing the best I can, Pippa. I need you to understand that. This private school is going to break our budget in the fall, but I know how important it is to you."

Pippa stifled a groan. As if she should be *so* grateful that her mum was sending her to a private prep. That was a basic necessity. She wanted to sing and dance like Jennifer Lopez. And you couldn't learn that by getting wanded down for metal objects in some knackered public school. To keep up in Miami, what Pippa really needed was new clothes, her own car, and endless bits of cash.

All of a sudden, thoughts of Annabelle Somerset, her best mate in London, crowded Pippa's mind, triggering a deep pang of sadness. She wondered what Annabelle was doing right now.

Before the scandal, the two girls had been inseparable— shopping like heiresses, going on chat rooms, having a right laugh about everything. Life was perfect. Pippa wondered if she'd ever be as happy as that again. And who wouldn't have been? They lived in a Soane and Lutyens-designed home with thirty-two bedrooms!

And now she was trapped in a riches-to-rags nightmare that seemed to have no end. To go from an English estate to a dodgy cottage with a single loo was enough to give anyone screaming gut-rot. It was as if God had decided to single her out for the tedious moral lesson of "less is more."

"I'm doing the best I can," Sophie said. "If money's an issue, then maybe you need to think about getting a job."

Pippa shut her eyes. Oh, how about that magic? Being forced into child slavery for a decent wad of spending money. What a pisser!

"Let's talk about this tomorrow," Sophie said. "I'm tired, and I have an early call in the morning."

Pippa refused to respond. She just lay there, wondering if there could be a bigger waste of sperm on the planet than her father. After all, he was the cause of the upheaval in their lives.

"Good night, sweetheart," Sophie said softly. "I love you." Her voice sounded so needy and forlorn, as if she only said the words to hear them boomerang.

Pippa caved instantly. "I love you, too, Mum."

And then Sophie stepped out of the room and shut the door quietly behind her.

More often than not, Pippa could be a royal pain. She knew this. But her mum loved her unconditionally just the same. And she loved her mum straight back.

Sophie had been an American college student studying abroad for a semester when she met Drummond Keith, a self-made commercial property developer with projects in London, New York, Paris, and Hong Kong. As a teenager, Pippa had lived out the tragic, bitter end to their romance. But she still loved the fairy-tale beginning.

Scrapbooks of their early years together captivated Pippa because seeing the photographs was no yawn. Her parents had been stunning in their youth, and she gazed upon them like Posh and Becks. Pippa felt wacky admitting this, but her dad had been a super hottie as a lad. It was no wonder her mum ditched school and never looked back at the States.

After a movie montage courtship and a countryside wedding, Pippa—their first and only child—had been born almost nine months to the first honeymoon night, spent in Greece on Christina Onassis's island.

The real trouble began several years into the marriage, when Drummond Keith's business became successful enough to earn him the privilege of high-leverage living. Sophie freely admitted to having seen early danger signs but was too young and naïve to shrewdly interpret them. Apparently, from the very beginning, inevitable clues of heartbreak had been there, bubbling beneath the surface—suspicions of philandering, occasional hell-raising . . . and reclusive addictions.

With his business going bang-on, Drummond went pogo like a total loon, spending money so fast that people thought he was scooping it out of the River Thames. There were new homes, cars, boats, a Learjet, a helicopter, gambling trips to

Las Vegas and Monte Carlo, parties that stretched on for entire weekends. And then the rumors started to circulate. About her father being a bum bandit. About the drugs. For a long time, Pippa and Sophie just went on with their lives, dismissing the talk as vicious gossip.

But when the behavior escalated to public humiliations, there was no room for denial. Her father had morphed into a degenerate. His homosexual dalliances became openly promiscuous. His cocaine habit became so sinister that he was an outright junkie. And his development company collapsed as he squandered millions of pounds and ignored important business affairs.

Then came the violent meltdown. Drummond—wrecked on coke and vodka—had been behind the wheel of his new Bentley when he hit a Vespa. He jumped out of the car, raged at the injured man for damaging his gleaming hubcaps, grabbed a tire iron from the trunk, and proceeded to beat the rider and his motor scooter completely senseless.

By this time Sophie had endured enough. She did *not* want to be anybody's put-upon wife. The only answer was to get out—in every sense of the word. And Pippa offered up no protest. At this point, she was suffering socially, suddenly isolated as the daughter of a coked-up knob-jockey nutter. Only Annabelle stuck by her during this horrific period, and even she'd grown increasingly distant.

With Drummond facing a labyrinth of lawsuits, massive debts, pending criminal charges, and frozen accounts, Sophie and Pippa barely escaped London with their lives. To raise cash, they set up a stall outside their estate and sold valuable things at knockdown prices. Pippa had cried as her huge collection of Chanel, Louis Vuitton, Prada, Hermès, Gucci, and Christian Dior bags got scooped up by bitchy ex-friends who laughed at her circumstances while walking off with their loot.

Deciding to move to Miami had been an easy call. Sophie had a job waiting there that would pay just enough to support her and Pippa. Though she never finished college and had no formal training, Sophie was a natural home design talent. Her approachable demeanor gave domestic workers, office staff, and young entry-level career strivers a comfort level about asking her advice on decorating their dingy little flats. A path began to show. Sophie found that she adored transforming living spaces on meager budgets. And she was good at it. Channel Four put up a deal to host her own program, then shut it down after three successful airings when the worst of the scandal crashed the front pages of the British press.

From out of the blue, an offer arrived to topline a new decorating show, *The Frugal Designer: South Beach Style*. The series was being launched by INT, a new cable network dedicated to all things interiors. It was a chance at a new life. Though it'd be a far different one. INT was in start-up mode, which meant salaries were modest at best, especially for Sophie Keith, who was an unproven commodity with American audiences. Still, it was a decent opportunity. So here they were, giving it a go in Miami.

Pippa's mobile rang, breaking her free from the so-recent painful past. It was Max. She picked up and blasted him straight off. "My mum read that text, you wanker!"

Max laughed. "Are you serious?"

"Yes!" Pippa confirmed. "I left my phone in the kitchen, and she came roaring into my room. Now she's insisting on meeting you before we can go out again."

Max groaned. "Shit. First Christina's mom, now yours. Am I losing my charm? Guess that means you can't hit a few clubs tonight."

Pippa gave her body a long, languid stretch, like a cat in the sun. "*Please.* I'm still recovering from last night."

"You just have to start drinking again," Max said, his voice ringing with an annoying authority and even more annoying pep. "It's the best way to deal."

"My mum's already in bed. She's not going to meet you tonight," Pippa said, punctuating the bad news with a lazy yawn.

"Sounds like you're in bed, too," Max said.

"I am. I'm *so* tired." Pippa yawned again. "How much did I drink last night?"

"I don't know. But it was enough to have you sucking off me and Dante before you passed out," Max said.

The flood tide of Pippa's shock collided with the breakwater of Max's unexpected words. "I did not!" Her denial was absolute. But then came the moment of dreadful doubt. She played back the previous evening on superspeed fast-forward in her mind. The missing moments worried her. Hardly a full-on blackout, but there were definitely some half memories to sort out.

"Why do you think I sent you that text?" Max went on. "Be proud, girl. You could suck the chrome off an exhaust pipe."

Pippa's heart banged in her chest. She bit down on her lip. Oh, God, could it be true? She wondered this for several long, terrible, torturous seconds.

And then Max started to laugh. "Gotcha!"

"You shitbag!" Pippa shouted. But then she found herself laughing with relief.

"For a minute there, you really thought you were the BJ queen of Star Island, didn't you?"

"I did not!" Pippa insisted. "Listen, if you and Dante chucked your muck last night, then it was the two of you cracking each other off. *I* had nothing to do with it."

Max's laughing thundered on. "Damn, I love the way you talk." One beat. "So what are you wearing?"

"Why?" Pippa asked.

"You said that you're in bed, right? Tell me what you've got on."

She hesitated. "Knickers and a little tee."

"What color?"

"White."

"Hmm. That sounds hot."

"Are you trying to have phone sex with me?"

"Not yet. We have to have real sex first. Phone sex comes later."

"Oh, really?" Pippa wondered. There was a challenge in her voice that told the Hollywood baby boy he stood no chance of getting a shag from her.

"Yes, really," Max fired back.

If there was a cockier lad on the planet, Pippa hadn't met him yet. "Well, I hope you don't get knob rot waiting for that day."

"Why? Because you're wet for Dante now?" Max tried to sound cool, but a hint of jealousy had crept into his tone.

"He's lush, but I don't fancy him. Not my type."

"You must not like mutts," Max said.

"What do you mean?" Pippa asked.

"He's half-Puerto Rican, half-black," Max explained.

"It's not that." His implication that she was prejudiced infuriated her. "God, you're such an asshole!"

Max laughed.

Pippa giggled. "You know, I thought he was going to beat seven shades of shit out of you last night."

"We were drunk," Max remarked easily. "No biggie."

"I can't even remember what started it."

"I talked a little trash about his mom. She's one of our maids. Maybe I should accuse her of stealing something."

Pippa was outraged. "Max!" Still, she found herself laughing. He was *so* incorrect.

"I know, I'm a dick. But that's why you'll end up banging me one day. Dante's too serious for you. I'll make you laugh, *and* I'll make you come."

"We're mates, Max," Pippa said earnestly. "I don't want to ruin that." She thought about how much she missed her friend Annabelle. She also thought about how nasty Vanity had been to her since she'd arrived. "Can I tell you something?"

"What?"

"You're the best mate I have in the world right now." As Pippa gave breath to those last words, her voice quivered with emotion.

"That's a sweet thing to say," Max said softly. Then he grew quiet, as if carefully choosing his next words. "But at the very least you've got to show me your tits."

"Max!" Pippa exclaimed. "I've never met a bigger pig in my life!"

He laughed.

Pippa laughed with him. She really did have a mate in Max. And it was a great feeling.

"Still tired?" he asked.

Pippa thought about it. "Not as much."

"Good. Get dressed. I'm coming to pick you up."

"What about my mum?" Pippa asked.

"Figure something out," Max told her. "There's always the window. That's a classic escape."

Pippa went through the motions of wavering, even

though ninety-nine percent of her had already decided to go along. "Just so you know, I don't have *any* cash."

"No worries. You can drink all night for free," Max said. "On one condition."

Pippa was already rolling her eyes. "And what might that be?"

"A flash of those tits."

Pippa shook her head, laughing at him. "Fine! I'll show you my puppies. But just this once." She hung up and rushed around, careful not to make too much noise. After all, her mum spent more hours crying at night than she did sleeping.

Memories of Pippa's huge walk-in closet at the London estate blistered her brain as she slid open the door to her new cramped storage space, hoping to find something to wear. Not much to choose from. Her finest pieces had been sold. She scowled at the warped top shelf and the bits of chipped paint that littered the floor. This place was a total hole. Meanwhile, Max and Vanity lived like a duke and duchess in their palatial homes. *So* unfair.

Pippa snatched one of the few designer frocks she had left—a great number by Ann Demeulemeester. It was a sexy, dangerously short distressed white cotton dress with shoulder straps as thin as dental floss. All the better for Pippa to show off her killer tan and flawless body.

She snatched her best and only pair of spike-heeled Manolo Blahniks and tiptoed to the loo, where she mussed her hair into a just-shagged mess with Dirt by Jonathan Product. Then she quickly applied mascara, swiped on some lip gloss, and—just for kicks—put on her John Richmond shades with VIVA emblazoned on one arm and RICH emblazoned on the other. Sunglasses at night. How brilliant. Finally, nosebleed sandals still in hand, she ducked out into the warm night to wait for Max.

The moon was out, lighting up the blackened blue of the sky and painting the palm trees in its glow. Pippa basked in the peaceful moment, alone here in the darkness, dreaming dreams as the fireflies twinkled. She shifted her bare feet, and a loose stone from a deep crack in the concrete lodged into her tender heel. Wincing at the pain, she slipped into her Manolos, a precious item she held back from those bitches who'd attacked the Keith family rummage sale like bloody vultures. Oh, God, she wanted money again. Fistfuls of cash. It'd make everything so much better.

From a distance, she heard the low rumble of Max's Porsche. The sound triggered a flicker of disappointment. Secretly, Pippa wanted to be by herself for a bit longer. But that wasn't in the cards. As every boy racer's auto fantasy approached, its headlights went dark, and the sports machine coasted to a stealthy, silent stop in front of her poor, pitiful shack. That's when a ripple of excitement did a somersault inside Pippa's stomach, telling her why she did the things she did. It was her own Girl's Guide to Getting Over a Family Holocaust.

Sneaking out.

Having a laugh.

Cockteasing boys.

Getting trashed.

Forgetting the past.

Pippa slid into the passenger seat, experiencing a sonic assault of "Pimpin' All Over the World" by Ludacris and Bobby Valentino. The interior cabin light was on, providing just enough illumination to give Max his thrill and to secure her credit line for the night.

Straps off. Dress down. No bra. Full view.

Max threw back his head in complete astonishment, staring at her perfectly proportioned beauties as if they were the unofficial eighth wonder of the world. Then, as if spellbound, his eyes lingered on the starfishlike scar a few inches underneath her left breast. He swallowed hard.

"Okay, show's over," Pippa chirped, pulling up her dress.

"How'd you get that scar?" Max asked.

"When I was born, my esophagus wasn't connected to my stomach, so I had to be operated on at two hours old," Pippa answered, feeling no shame or self-consciousness. The distinguishing mark belonged to her, and she was right proud of it.

For a prolonged moment, Max gazed at her with genuine fascination and obvious lust. "Goddamn, that's hot. It makes me want to nail you even more."

Pippa laughed. "Stop being such a perv and drive!"

Max wiggled his eyebrows and floored it, roaring the Porsche engine to maximum revs.

Pippa glanced back, half wondering if the ruckus had been loud enough to wake up her mum, then dismissed the thought altogether. Too late now anyway. Tomorrow she'd deal. Tonight she'd party.

"We were just here," Pippa whined, as Max led the charge toward the door police at Mynt.

She wanted desperately to hit B.E.D., a club with loads of mattresses. A girl could just lie about and get waited on like a princess. And if she felt like snogging a dreamy lad, then she could do so to her heart's content behind the billowy white curtains. Total heaven.

"Every night here is different," Max informed her. "And it's only our first stop." As he approached a bulky bouncer, Max offered him a cool nod, then watched the man work fast to remove the rope barrier, his free arm splayed out wide to separate the son of a famous movie star from the nobodies lined up with hopeful dreams of getting inside.

This made Pippa wonder if Max Biaggi Jr. had ever waited for *anything* in his life. And a gut instinct told her that—besides a shag with her, for which the bloke would be waiting forever—the answer was no.

Max walked in, cruised in, strutted in. He gave off nuclear attitude. Like he owned the club lock, stock, and liquor supply.

From the power speakers, Mariah Carey cooed a lazy hip-hop groove, telling the party crowd to "Shake It Off."

Pippa scanned the long, narrow hot zone, her eyes adjusting to the glossy green décor accented with earth-toned couches where the pretty, prettier, and prettiest people hung out, chilled out, and made out.

"Check it," Max said, gesturing across the room.

Pippa glanced over to see rocker Tommy Lee tattooed, trashed, and tangled up in a gaggle of suntanned Miami beach girls. One word: *Yuck.*

"Show him what you showed me, and maybe he'll let you see it in the flesh," Max said.

Pippa gave him a confused look. "See what?"

"His dick," Max said. "It's supposed to be, like, a foot long or something. Unless the camera adds inches or something."

She pulled a face. "Not interested. Apparently, *you* are, though."

Max laughed, sidled up to the bar for two Red Bull and Levels, and returned, looking bulletproof in a place so jammed with beautiful people that even the superattractive could develop self-doubt. But not Max.

And not Pippa, either. God had blessed her with an amazing figure—long legs, a tiny waist, breasts that could make the lads cry for their mums, slightly broad shoulders, and a tummy so pancake flat that it concaved a bit, no matter how many bags of M&M candies she wolfed down. Of course, she still had body issues. What teenage girl didn't? Pippa secretly longed to be shorter, like some of the girls in her ballet class back in London.

"God, I can't believe I'm cranking it up again," Pippa remarked, as she accepted the offering from Max, downed the vodka, and chased it with the Red Bull.

"Never give in to a hangover," Max said. "It's accepting defeat."

"Oh, thanks for the tip, gladiator," Pippa chortled. Then she passed him her empty containers, puckering up her lips into a beautiful pout charade. "More." One beat. "Pretty please?"

There was a second drink. Followed by a third. And when the fourth cocktail arrived on the beat drop of "Lose Control" by Missy Elliott with Ciara and Fat Man Scoop, Pippa felt an uninhibited buzz going strong. She smiled at Max. She smiled to herself.

The futuristic techno sample from Cybotron bent the air of the packed club. Suddenly, the hard-charging rhythm kicked in, whipping bodies into a frenzy. Even Max was dancing—in that ultracool way that only some guys could pull off.

But Pippa didn't hold back. She let her body go loose over the beat, wiggling her ass, throwing back her head, laughing and laughing, shimmy-shaking in a show that proved to every other female in the special orbit of Mynt that a true dancer was present and accounted for.

"Shake what yo mama gave ya, girl!" Max hooted and hollered.

Pippa grooved between Max's stretched-out legs, pointing at him, her long finger aimed like a gun between his happy, bleary, wide-open eyes. Spinning around, she dipped low, just barely grinding against his crotch, bringing out a caged howl from the rich brat of Star Island that made him sound like the guest of honor at the wildest bachelor party on earth.

The music flowed within her, and Pippa felt a strange sense of total surrender. In fact, her body didn't belong to her anymore. It was a slave to the rhythm.

Max's eyes were all over her. So were other eyes. Male ones. Females ones, too. Mynt was full to bursting. And a girl with too much booze on the brain who looked like her and moved like this was a clap of party thunder in the night.

"Dance on the bar, baby," a male voice yelled.

Pippa turned.

It wasn't Max. It was Tommy Lee.

Several more people screamed their agreement.

Even though Pippa felt in charge of the situation, all freedom had gone away. They wanted to watch her dance. She wanted them to see her dance. And as the raw power of mutual wish fulfillment raced through her bloodstream, she negotiated the climb onto the bar with eager assistance from the crowd buried there at least ten-deep.

"Rump shakin' both wayz/Make u do a double take."

The Missy Elliott sound track ruled her body as it

rocked to the beat in a series of intrinsically choreographed moves.

Sexy.

Seductive.

Sultry.

By miracle alone, her stiletto-heeled Manolos clung to the wet bar as she spun, kicked, and twisted before the salivating strangers. It was a dull night for the Miami party posse . . . until Pippa Keith gave them murder on the dance floor.

"Get it crunk and wired / Wave ya hands scream louda."

She shook her hair from side to side, pushing her hips forward as her hands found the upper-outer quandrants of her buttocks and pumped her midtorso back and forth, punctuating the gyration with a flash of tongue over her lips.

Pippa vibed on the energy of the crowd, proudly holding herself up before the feasting night eyes. Her covered breasts canopied over them. Suddenly, she was overcome by the strangest feeling that this wasn't her playing exhibitionist on the bar. It was a fantasy, an image, a persona, something that could be clicked on and off whenever she wanted. She knew that. And the realization gave her an erotic charge. Because she was in control . . . she was powerful.

To prove it, Pippa lifted her dress just high enough to reveal the pure white silk of her panties. Hooking a finger into the elastic didn't just tease the dumb lads sweating her every move. It *killed* them.

Max was on life support.

Tommy Lee was dying.

And the man who reached up to slip a hundred-dollar bill under the band of her panties was six feet under.

But as she slayed the men beneath her, Pippa had never felt so alive.

From: Mimi

I'm fielding calls from 2 very pissed off
sponsors because you blew off their events.
Call me!

11:48 am 6/22/05

chapter seven

Vanity woke up feeling awful. Her head was pounding, her face was burdened with makeup from two nights ago, and, amazingly, her body still thrummed (and not in a good way) with sexual aftershocks from the interlude with J.J.

Oh, God, why had she allowed herself to be used that way? It was the same cycle repeating itself. While in the moment, hooking up seemed like the fun thing to do. But the hours that followed were a different story altogether. Because that's when she felt like a dumb slut.

With a sudden, anxiety-fueled alert, Vanity rose up and scrambled for her Sidekick II. The abrupt movement sent her reeling. Still, she soldiered on, jabbing at the keyboard to ignore Mimi's message and speed dial Dr. Cleo Parker's office. As always, it rang straight to voicemail.

"Dr. Parker, this is Vanity." Her voice sounded late-night hoarse. So obviously the result of brutal partying and subsequent crashing, especially since the clock was about to tick over to noon. "I'm running late, but I'll be there."

She dressed quickly, the same People's Liberation jeans from two days ago, a white ribbed cotton tank, and a lightweight, coral-colored Juicy Couture hoodie. There was no time to shower, to wash her face, or to even attempt camouflaging the wild life damage of the last thirty-six hours. All Vanity could do was simply brush her teeth to rid her taste buds of that horrible trench mouth sensation.

She dashed madly out of her bedroom, realizing with a panic that flooring it to Dr. Parker's office—assuming no traffic—would get her there with only twenty minutes left to go on their scheduled session.

As Vanity tore out of the house, she passed Mercedes and Gunnar. They were jumping up and down to a concert DVD of the children's music group Hi-Five. She gave them a vague wave, ignored Lala completely, and made a beeline for the garage.

A quick turn of the SmartKey and her Capri-blue Mercedes SL500 Roadster purred to life. Seconds later, the stereo blew up, rocking her solar plexus. It was still set on party volume. But she let it stay there, needing some noise to crash into her head and shake loose the fog of the Ambien pills that had knocked her into a comalike sleep that lasted a full day.

XM Radio ruled. Vanity kept her tuner perpetually locked onto Channel 202, High Voltage, which carried *The Opie and Anthony Show,* a take-no-prisoners raunchy comedyfest with the hosts and their sidekick, comedian Jim Norton.

Any subject was fair game to these guys, and the nonstop banter—blisteringly profane and shockingly sexual—never failed to leave Vanity in a jaw-dropping state of disbelief. Howard Stern was so over. Opie and Anthony were the new destroyers of good taste in America.

At the press of a button, the convertible top went down. Vanity cruised the back roads, then opened up the engine to race along Ocean Drive. The sun blazed like an angry ball of fire. Even the sea-salt breeze couldn't provide relief. Beads of sweat began to form between her shoulder blades, and a little damp patch had already pooled between her breasts.

But Vanity couldn't blame the Miami summer. Not when she was still bleeding tequila from her pores. The odor sickened her. God, she felt like a nasty, smelly whore. What a way to start the day. Healthy living. Good times. Yeah, right.

Her spirits were buoyed somewhat by the radio show. Vanity cackled as Jim Norton went on a ferocious rant about fat girls. It was cruel and inhuman . . . but it was still funny as hell. This made her wonder if she might be part of that new breed of young woman—the female chauvinist pig, the kind who sees *Girls Gone Wild* antics as acts of empowerment, the kind who makes boys blush in bars when she tells a joke dirtier than theirs.

Glancing up, Vanity noticed a group of pelicans swooping across the royal blue sky in perfect fighter plane formation. If only she could join them. Go wherever they were going. How blissful that would be. To fly away on the ultimate escape.

She barely heard the ring of her cellular over the hilarious shock jock / frat boy bullshit. Twisting down the volume, she checked the screen. It was Mimi. And no doubt a very pissed-off Mimi.

Reluctantly, Vanity picked up. "Hello?"

"What the *hell* is going on?" Mimi demanded. "I called you a million times yesterday. The Sony people are furious. I can't believe you. Katee K's party had massive coverage, you never showed up, and now I'm hearing that you got drunk at the Surfcomber and went upstairs with Jayson James!"

Hearing the gory details out loud brought on a quick and palpable shame. Vanity could actually feel it, as hot as the sun on her face. How could she explain herself? She'd done something stupid. And for reasons that were more stupid. At this moment, silence seemed like the best response.

Mimi sighed the sigh of the irritated. "Can't you see that I'm on a business call?" she shrieked. "Work on my ass, okay?"

Vanity laughed a little. "Where are you?"

"Getting an airbrush tan," Mimi snapped. "Listen to me. Jayson James is *not* in your league. His career is going down the crapper. The guy is a total loser. Everybody knows that his bulge was stuffed for the Hilfiger ads, and now everybody's over him. Come on! If you want to go slumming, just hook up with one of the hot guys from *The Real World*. I can't promise that you won't get chlamydia, but at least you'd be associating with the kind of pseudo-celebrity garbage that might make an interesting photo op."

Suddenly, Vanity thought of Dante. This brought a secret smile to her lips. Hmm. What would Mimi think about him? If a semifamous male model was incurring her wrath now, then she would definitely go ballistic over Dante's credentials—son of a housekeeper, swim coach to little tots, wannabe rapper. Oh, yes. Mimi Blair would *die* over that résumé.

"Enough of that," Mimi went on. "We all make mistakes. I slept with a Backstreet Boy once. Shoot me."

Vanity laughed. "I didn't know that. Which one?"

"I'll never tell. But let's just say I figured things out quicker than Paris Hilton did. Okay, on to business. *InStyle* wants you for a sidebar feature on what's inside your purse."

"Seriously?"

"I know it sounds retarded, but they've budgeted a location photo shoot, and the interview is just a ten-minute phoner."

"Well, I better change handbags," Vanity said. "The one with me right now has my thong from the other night inside it."

"Yes, bitch. *Please* change purses. I'll call you with the details." Mimi signed off.

Vanity punched the accelerator as she turned onto Michigan Avenue, screeching into the private parking deck at 1680. Dr. Cleo Parker owned space on the top floor at this address, one of the newest and most expensive office towers in South Beach.

At the insistence of her father, Vanity had been seeing Dr. Parker once a week for the last six months. In the beginning, she bitterly resented being forced to go. First, why would he suddenly believe that she needed a psychiatrist? Did Simon St. John think she was crazy? And second, the whole idea just seemed like another lazy attempt at outsourcing his role as a parent. Basically, the man had neither the time nor the interest in dealing with the emotional minefields that went along with raising a teenage daughter. So why not farm her out to some shrink?

No matter her initial wariness, Vanity quickly realized that therapy was something she should've sought out long before. Finally, she had a place to be heard. Dr. Parker actually listened to her problems and fears and dreams and desires—without standing in judgment (as her father so often did) or interrupting to blather on about her own issues (as was the case with so many friends).

Vanity's hour with Dr. Parker was about Vanity. Exclusively. And no aspect of her celebrity or family wealth impressed the therapist. If anything, during the course of a session, Vanity's most fame game-worthy points of reference merely drew blank stares from the woman.

But that's not to say that Dr. Parker was clueless. Quite the contrary. Her bullshit detector was a finely tuned instrument of such drop-dead accuracy that Vanity couldn't get away with anything. Not even the slightest attempts at deception or avoidance. And if she tried, Dr. Parker would call her out on it every time.

For this reason, the elevator rides up to her office stirred up the butterflies in her stomach. Intense therapy was a frightening gauntlet. It meant uncovering the ugliest demons and confronting them head-on. Even now, half a year into the journey, Vanity found herself fighting a private war whenever she darkened the doorway of Dr. Parker's inner sanctum. How deep would the psychiatrist encourage her to go today? And how much would Vanity be willing to reveal? The nagging sense that holding back might render the entire process a waste of time always prodded her to share more.

She stepped into the reception area and paced the floor, anxiously flipping through the new issue of *Architectural Digest* but taking in none of the content. It was merely something to do.

Absently, she gazed out the floor-to-ceiling windows onto Lincoln Road. Vanity's guts were knotted. She tapped out a nervous rhythm with one foot. God, she couldn't shake that filthy feeling. Right now she would be willing to crawl two miles over broken glass for a shower.

She slipped into one of the glossy black Louis Ghost chairs and tried to relax. It struck Vanity as odd that Dr.

Parker's décor was so modern—the sleek Philippe Starck furniture, the bold color accent pieces, the Andy Warhol original on the wall. The latter was one of the artist's famous Marilyn Monroe portraits. How appropriate. The tragic star's reliance on psychotherapy had become the stuff of Hollywood legend.

Staring at the painting, Vanity's mind shot into hyperdrive on all things Monroe—her sad childhood, her difficulty forming female friendships that lasted, her powerful sexuality and the way people used her for it, her endless problems with men, and, ultimately, her early death. There were disturbing similarities between the girl in the chair and the woman on the wall. Suddenly, a voice inside Vanity's head asked quite clearly, Could I end up like that?

The door to Dr. Cleo Parker's inner office opened, and she stood there beaming a welcoming smile. "Hello, Vanity." Her voice was soft and comforting. She was a tiny woman— barely five feet tall—with a yoga addict's body and short black hair speckled with hints of gray that she didn't bother to hide by making frequent trips to a colorist.

"I'm sorry," Vanity said as she stepped inside the dimly lit room. "I don't think I've ever been this late before."

"It's okay," Dr. Parker said soothingly. "My one o'clock appointment canceled, so we're fine on time." She closed the door behind her.

Vanity waited for the cue.

Dr. Parker expanded her arms.

Vanity moved in to accept her embrace. It was a long,

warm, nurturing, maternal hug. She got one at the beginning of her session, and she got one at the end. Sometimes she felt like it was the most healing aspect of showing up each week.

The truth was, simple affection often felt alien to Vanity. Her mother had always been aloof, more concerned about her favorite substance of the moment than her own daughter. And even though Simon St. John used to make Vanity feel adored with smothering hugs and silly kisses, all those displays had ceased to exist years ago, around the same time that other men began to take notice of her beauty and budding sexuality. Almost overnight, she went from daddy's little girl to stranger, lucky to get so much as an awkward one-arm embrace around the shoulder. This made Vanity feel dirty, and it triggered a pattern of seeking out affection on any terms . . . and often settling for the wrong kind.

Bottom line: Guys wanting sex would never fill the void for a girl missing something in her life. God, it seemed so ridiculously simple. If you were longing to feel loved, then stay away from horny jerks. Because time after time, they would only leave you feeling worse. Vanity knew this. J.J. was proof positive. To a lesser degree, Max was, too. And there had been others. So why didn't she know better by now?

As was the custom, Dr. Parker broke the embrace, took possession of Vanity's hands, and gazed directly into her eyes while asking, "How are you?"

"Terrible," Vanity admitted. She took her position on the Eames sofa, sinking into the quilted black leather.

Dr. Parker settled in opposite her. "Why do you say that?"

Vanity sighed. For the moment, she just answered the question with a diffident shrug.

"You reek of alcohol," Dr. Parker said. It was more matter-of-fact observation than character judgment. "And it doesn't appear that you've showered. Maybe we should start with where you were last night."

Vanity inspected her nails and made a mental note to schedule a manicure. "Sleeping. But the other night I went out with J.J."

"You've seen him before, right?" Dr. Parker inquired.

Vanity nodded.

"He's the model?"

"Yeah, that's him." She paused a beat. "We went to a party at a hotel. It was lame. I ended up drinking a lot. Then he took me up to his room. He smokes pot. I don't, but I got stoned from just being in the same space. One thing led to another, and we had sex. When I woke up the next morning, he was gone. So I went home to crash."

Dr. Parker nodded thoughtfully, betraying no disapproval. "How did that make you feel?"

"Like an idiot slut," Vanity said.

"As I recall, this is familiar ground with J.J. He's made you feel like this before."

Vanity rolled her eyes. "I guess that means I have a learning disability."

Dr. Parker smiled ruefully. "Not necessarily. When it

comes to men, I think we're all slow learners. It's common for women to think, Next time this guy will be different. But he rarely is."

Vanity shook her head. "It wasn't that way with me. When J.J. called to ask me out and I said yes, I *knew* what it would be. I knew it would happen. And that's what kills me. I didn't want to go out with him. I didn't want to go to the party. I didn't want to have sex. Yet I said yes to it all. And then I drank too much, so I'd be too wasted to second-guess anything."

"Why do you think that is?" Dr. Parker asked.

"Because at the time I felt worthless." Vanity blinked back a tear, then wiped her eye with the back of her hand. "And putting myself out there to be used . . . I don't know . . . it seemed like a good enough way to get through the night."

"And was it?"

Vanity felt a wave of emotion rise up. "No." She covered her face as the tears came in full force.

Dr. Parker reached over to pass her a handful of tissues. "It's okay. This is a safe place to get these things out."

Vanity blotted her eyes and blew her nose, trying to pull herself together.

"Let's talk about these feelings of worthlessness," Dr. Parker said quietly. "What was going on to put you in that state of mind?"

Vanity hesitated. "I met this guy," she began slowly. "I was doing publicity for a club, and he was there. I noticed him right away. Which is rare. I mean . . . guys usually notice me first. That's how it works. But not this time. Anyway, we had this intense conversation. His father died in Desert Storm, and he had this sweet tattoo of his name, rank, and serial number on his arm. I don't know. I just felt this connection between us. It was a crazy, instant attraction. That's never happened to me before. This guy didn't get off on the fact that I was famous. If anything, that was a mark against me. It annoyed me, but at the same time I thought it was kind of cool. So as it turns out, he's transferring to my school in the fall for his senior year. He's into music. He wants to be a rapper." Vanity rolled her eyes skyward. "I think we have enough of those, don't you? Why doesn't anybody want to learn Arabic dialects and go work for the CIA?"

Dr. Parker smiled. "What's his name?"

"Dante," Vanity said. "And get this—he also turned up as the swim coach for Mercedes and Gunnar."

Dr. Parker's brow lifted. "Small world."

"I think he planned it that way. You know, to get near my father and slip him a demo or something. So we had a second encounter at our pool. Of course, my dad was there acting like a complete asshole, which is the only way he knows how to act. But this guy, Dante, was talking to me face-to-face, and I could actually sense him factoring the math in his head. You know, working out the equation."

Dr. Parker gave her a quizzical look. "What equation?"

"Me," Vanity clarified. "I picked up on the fact that he

was doing the calculations. Was I worth the trouble? As a potential girlfriend. Or even as a piece of ass." Her voice went up an octave as she bitterly sang, *"Apparently not."*

"If he lost his father in Desert Storm, I assume he's from a working-class background," Dr. Parker said.

"His mother's a maid at Max's house."

"Do you think it's possible that you're reading too much into this?" Dr. Parker ventured. "Your father is a rich and powerful man. You said yourself that he was acting out. Perhaps Dante was just intimidated by the surroundings."

Vanity leaned in to emphasize her point. "I saw it, Dr. Parker. I felt it, too. What he was thinking might as well have been running across his forehead like the headline updates on CNN." In a huff, she leaned back against the sofa. "Whatever. Dante can kiss Simon St. John's ass until his lips are raw. It doesn't matter. My father will *never* help him. He hates daydreamers who accost him with unsolicited demos. Somebody's always trying to give him a CD or DAT—valets, waiters, car wash guys, pushy parents. He tosses all of them without even a first listen."

Dr. Parker observed her with a penetrating stare. She allowed a single beat to pass. "Let's get back to this sense of unworthiness. Are you saying that Dante's ambivalence made you feel that way?"

"In part," Vanity responded glumly. "It just put me in a mood. I went to my room. J.J. called. And I was, like, whatever."

Dr. Parker nodded thoughtfully. "We've talked before about the importance of cultivating stronger friendships with girls. Any progress on that front?"

"Funny you should bring that up. I probably should've gone shopping with Pippa the other day."

"Why didn't you?"

"I don't know . . . she gets on my nerves. Is that a good enough reason?"

Dr. Parker considered this. "It can be."

Vanity found herself struggling to conjure up other examples of efforts to make female friends. "There's another girl—Christina. But she's kind of weird. She's an *artist*. And she stares a lot. It sort of makes me uncomfortable."

There was an extended silence.

Vanity felt compelled to come clean. "I'm so much harder on girls than I am on guys. That's part of my problem, I guess. I'll forgive a guy almost anything and just convince myself to accept him where he is, no matter how big a dickhead he's been. Take J.J. He treated me like a road whore the last time we were together, but I glossed over that and went out with him again." Vanity shook her head. "I don't know why I'm this way. Maybe it's because my mother's so screwed-up. Maybe it's because most girls are jealous and think that I'm going to steal their boyfriends. It's just always been easier to be friends with guys."

"How is it easier?"

"I don't have to try as hard," Vanity admitted. "If I feel

like being a bitch, it's no big deal. Guys won't go anywhere. It's always about the sex that they had before and want again or the sex that they're trying to get." She sighed heavily. "Everyone has this image of me, you know? I'm the famous hot girl in the magazines who decides what's cool. To them, it's all perfect. 'Ooh, look at Vanity St. John. She's got money, friends to party with every night, an awesome car.'" She waved a dismissive hand through the air. "Most of the time, I feel like that girl is someone else. There's this public image of me that's totally together. That's who people see. That's who they're drawn to. But then there's the real me. And that girl's a complete mess." The twisted irony made her smile. "Guys really aren't insightful or observant, though. They don't pick up on that. Their deepest thought is more like, Man, is it just me, or do her tits look bigger today?"

Dr. Parker smiled.

Vanity laughed a little, pleased with her joke and grateful for the moment of levity. "I guess my fear is that if I allow girls to get close, they'll sense that about me."

"Why does that scare you?"

"Because I'm afraid that they won't like the real me, the girl with the insecurities who cries alone in her room all the time. I can see some bitch turning on me and telling everyone that I'm a phony. It's not worth the drama."

"You're not alone, Vanity," Dr. Parker said. "You're not the only girl out there with an ongoing image campaign that feels false. Yours is amplified by being in the media spotlight, but there are lots of girls who do the same thing day in and day out. They try to be perfect. They muzzle their emotions. They hide interests or opinions that might make them stand out. All of this is done because they want to stay connected. But it has the opposite effect. The most disconnected girls are the ones who silence their inner selves."

Vanity really listened to Dr. Parker, and this concentration provided a moment of epiphany. She parted her lips to speak, then thought better of it.

"Don't hold back," Dr. Parker said. "We're doing good work here. What were you going to say?"

"I was in Bal Harbour last week . . . and everywhere I looked I saw tourists. You can instantly pick them out with their bad clothes and fanny packs. There's this sense about them, though. It's like they have no control over where they're going. Do you know what I mean? It's whatever the guide-book says, or their travel agent, or their friends who came to Miami last year. Sometimes . . . that's how I feel . . . like a dumb tourist in my own life."

"Why do you think that is?"

"Because I hold so much back, and I keep so much inside. It's, like, all this time is going by, and there's a life going on, but I'm just a visitor. It's the strangest thing."

Dr. Parker gave her a curious look.

"How does that make you feel?" Dr. Parker asked.

Vanity considered the question. "It makes me sad."

"What kind of sadness? Describe it for me."

Vanity tried to isolate the emotion. "It's a feeling of loss, I guess. Sort of like I'm mourning a person that I used to be."

Dr. Parker's attention was total. "Go on."

"When I was younger, I remember having such a strong sense of myself. Oh, God, I was fearless. I had no problem saying whatever I thought or felt. If something was fake, I called it on the spot. I danced. I played soccer. I did gymnastics. I didn't care anything about boys. I laughed until I cried with my girlfriends. I felt secure in the fact that my father loved me, and I thought that connection would last forever."

"What happened to that little girl?" Dr. Parker asked gently.

"She died a long time ago," Vanity said.

From: Max

Pool party at the shore club. Can u roll or
do u have 2 mow a lawn? lmao.

1:51 pm 6/23/05

chapter eight

four-year-old Jovi Kelley was screaming blue murder . . . and so far he only had two feet ankle deep in the water. It was going to be a long summer with this kid.

But being stuck in a pool all day beat the shit out of bussing tables at Tony Roma's, which is what Dante had been doing before landing the SafeSplash job.

"It's okay, little man, it's okay," Dante assured him, his voice soothing but not too coddling. He lifted Jovi back onto the dry land of the coquina deck, a whitish-gray coral stone with natural fissures and fossilized shells.

Just as Jovi's terror began to subside, his father came rushing out of the main house in a panic. "I heard him crying!" Rob Kelley exclaimed, his tone equal parts concern and accusation.

"Everything's cool," Dante said. "He's just nervous. Isn't that right, little man?"

At first, Jovi managed an affirmative nod, but then he rushed into his father's arms, clung to him like a koala bear, and proceeded to bawl louder than a colicky baby.

Rob Kelley smothered the boy with kisses and stroked his back tenderly, cooing, "You don't have to go in the scary water if you don't want to, Jovi. Do you want to go inside for a snack? Do you want to watch a show? You know what? For being such a big boy today, I'm going to take you to the toy store and let you pick out anything you want."

"Okay," Jovi mumbled. And then he started sucking his thumb.

"Last summer we went through *four* swimming coaches," Rob explained. "He can't get past the fear. We just have to let him ease into this on his own time."

Dante merely nodded. Jesus Christ, this kid didn't stand a chance in life with Mr. Mommy at the controls.

Rob Kelley was the do-nothing husband of Naomi Kelley, the new It girl in Hollywood, thanks to her breakout star turn in *Pink Hard Hat,* a fluffy comedy about a pampered wife who starts a rival construction business to get back at a cheating ex. It was pretty much *Legally Blonde* on a building site. But the Monday after the movie's first big weekend at the box office, Naomi's price skyrocketed to fifteen million a picture.

Ka-ching. That explained Naomi and Rob's megabucks lifestyle. They lived in a mansion inside a gated community on Hibiscus Island, an oasis crammed with prime real estate and only accessible by car via the MacArthur Causeway. Dante figured that the pool installation alone must've run at least half a mil. He'd never seen a backyard water hole so tricked out.

It was a massive rectangular structure lined with reflective iridescent glass tiles. On one side, the pool dipped into a grotto surrounded by palm trees. An active jet spray in the bottom created the illusion of a hot spring. On the other side, the reef steps—imbedded with a Baja Bubbler that allowed for water spa massages—led into a sunken bar lined with floating stools.

Of course, the main attraction was the underwater volcano, triggered by a system below the surface that spurted a rush of air into the pool's shallow end. The water effect was intensified by a light in the center of activity that alternated from blazing orange to lava red.

As if all that wasn't enough, the pool also featured two infinity edges *and* an underwater sound system, which right now was pumping Power 96 and the exotic island beat of Rihanna's "Pon de Replay." Shit. To be Naomi Kelley's house husband. Not a bad gig if you could get it.

But Dante had some serious issues with Rob. First, he hated the way Jovi got cosseted like a fragile lamb. The kid was four years old going on two! The boy should have a little daredevil in him by now. And second, Dante was creeped out by the looks Rob sent in his direction. It felt like the man was openly cruising him. Poor Naomi. She was hot as hell and had lucked into a major movie career. Too bad she screwed up and married a wife instead of a husband.

"Theresa!" Rob bellowed sharply.

The nanny came running, and she was no Lala in the looks department. Jovi's caretaker was the female version of the *Super Size Me* guy, only she'd obviously never bothered to stop the fast-food-for-every-meal experiment.

"Take Jovi inside and fix him a snack," Rob barked, transferring the boy into Theresa's ample arms. "He's had enough of the pool for today."

"Yes, Mr. Kelley," the nanny responded dutifully, her voice almost robotic. There was a blank expression in her eyes, too, a giveaway for the kind of soul death that occurs when you spend your life slaving away for rich assholes who don't treat you like a whole person.

Dante knew that look. Now and then he saw it on the face of his own mother, Vanessa Medina. Granted, her position at the Biaggi spread on Star Island was probably her best job yet, but it was still cleaning toilets for a living. Grand or modest, mansion or trailer, at the end of the day, other people's shit was other people's shit.

Rob Kelley lingered, waiting for his son's swimming instructor to exit the pool. And the moment Dante emerged from the water, Rob's gaze locked onto a certain target, taking in an eyeful of Dante's package, boldly appreciative of the way his wet suit had gathered at the crotch.

Dante adjusted himself and zapped a glare over to Rob that translated, "Man, I'll not only kick your closet-case ass, but I'll show your wife what she's been missing while you're recovering at the hospital."

In the way that only people with millions in the bank can, Rob betrayed no embarrassment. He just tracked his eyes up a bit to obsess over Dante's six-pack abdominals. "You know, Naomi's in Toronto shooting a new film."

"Really? What's the project?" Better to fake interest and make like an IMDB addict than piss off the guy. After all, if Dante was Jovi's *fifth* swim coach, then there could easily be a sixth showing up tomorrow. And he needed this job. The pay was great, and the hours freed him up at night to party or work on his music.

"Life on Mars," Rob answered. "It's a sci-fi thriller."

"That sounds cool," Dante remarked casually, gathering his things from the Casatta hand-crafted bronze deck chaise.

"She's there for the next four months, so this pool isn't getting a lot of use," Rob went on. "You should come by at night sometime. The volcano looks incredible then. You'd love it."

Dante gave him a noncommittal nod and started out. "Same time tomorrow for Jovi?"

"Sure," Rob said, falling into step beside him. "He looks forward to the lessons. It might not seem that way, but believe me, you're doing great with him."

Dante grinned. "Thanks." One beat. "It might help if you

didn't stick close by for the next lesson. Let me test Jovi's fears. I think he's braver than you give him credit for. He wants to tackle that water. I can see it in his eyes."

"Sounds like a plan," Rob said, slapping a hand onto Dante's shoulder and allowing it to remain there longer than straight male manners allowed.

As they were passing a seating area on the deck, Dante spotted a shiny object on the coquina surface underneath a coffee table. He bent down to retrieve it, shocked to discover that it was a watch. And not just any watch. This was a platinum timepiece iced out with dense diamond crust on the band and bezel. Major bling. "Damn," Dante murmured, passing his find over to Rob. "Did you know this was out here?"

Rob held the watch in his hands and pulled a face. "Naomi and I went on a buying binge after her first big movie deal. Let's just say some bad decisions were made." He laughed a little. "This watch would be one of them. I never wear it. But it's an Iceman original."

Dante whistled his recognition. Iceman was the nickname for jeweler Chris Aire, the self-made cat who outfitted the earlobes, necks, wrists, and fingers of Eminem, 50 Cent, Nelly, Shaq, Chris Webber, and others. He even designed a set of platinum teeth for the rapper called Baby. "That's a fine piece of ice, man," Dante praised. "You should show it off."

For a long second, Rob Kelley stared at him. And then he

wordlessly handed the watch back to Dante. "Finders keepers. You take it."

The crushed ice felt like it was burning the skin raw on Dante's hand. But it was a hot potato that he didn't want to pass on. Finally, though, he came to his senses. "Are you crazy, man?" he asked, making a move to give it back.

Rob held up both hands in mock surrender, refusing to accept the gesture. "No. Take it," he insisted.

"I can't . . . this thing must be worth at least—"

"We didn't pay retail," Rob cut in. "Naomi drives a hard bargain. She cuts a deal on everything."

Dante stood there, knowing instinctively how wrong this was, yet at the same time feeling a weakening in his resolve to do the right thing. In fact, he flirted with the idea of trying on the watch for size, just for a cheap thrill.

"You should try it on," Rob suggested.

Dante looked up. Was this guy reading his mind?

"Go on," Rob encouraged.

Reluctantly, Dante slipped the watch over his wrist and locked the bracelet into place. *Shit.* It fit like a dream. It looked good. And it felt even better.

"Hey," Rob said with considerable nonchalance, "if you don't take it off my hands, I might just end up giving it to the gardener."

Dante stared down at the awesome piece adorning his wrist. The ice gleamed brilliantly in the sunlight. God, it made him feel ten feet tall to wear something like this. Sorry, bitches. Diamonds are a *guy's* best friend, too. He imagined the Iceman in his West Coast jewelry lab, setting the stones himself, doing it for the love of the art, not for the money.

Dante thought about the two hundred dollars he'd won from Max in the poker game. That would hardly pay for a speck of diamond dust, but it was something. Besides, Rob Kelley needed to know straight up that Dante wouldn't be trading out body for bling.

Then another thought came to mind. He'd really intended to set that cash aside for studio time. Cutting a quality demo for Simon St. John was top priority. But then again, fronting serious ice would get him noticed by players in the business who mattered—name producers, in-demand musicians, popular DJs. If they knew from the jump that Dante Medina knew how to roll, then connections would get locked and loaded faster. And it was all about connections.

"I can't just take your watch, man," Dante said. "I gotta pay you something for it . . . *in cash.*"

"I won't take your money," Rob told him. "Just teach Jovi how to swim. That's all the payment I need." He paused a beat. "And one more thing. Promise me that you'll come over some night and check out the volcano. Deal?" He extended a hand.

A strong foreboding told Dante that he'd end up regretting this arrangement. But he gave Rob's hand a firm grip and shook on it anyway.

•   •   •

Twenty minutes later, Dante's car stalled on the MacArthur Causeway. His Honda's CHECK ENGINE light had flashed, and just a few miles after that, the motor killed completely.

He went through what troubleshooting he knew how to do, but none of it seemed linked to the problem. It was mid-afternoon, and the sun blazed down with no mercy. He was practically sweating blood on this boiling side of the road as vehicles speeded past, ignoring his situation. People stopped for hot girls in expensive convertibles, not mixed-race dudes in raggedy used Civics.

Shit. Damn. Motherfu—

His cellphone chimed with the signal for an incoming text. He read Max's smart-ass message and ignored it for the moment to dial up his regular running buddy, Vince, hoping for a quick rescue.

His friend picked up with a gruff, "Yo."

"Hey, man, can you pick me up on the causeway? My car just busted."

"Hell no! I'm in the middle of a shift," Vince snapped.

Dante groaned. Vince worked as an assistant manager at a Subway sandwich shop in Key Biscayne and hated every minute of it. During the summer, he regularly put in more than fifty hours a week for crap pay. "Shit. My mom's working, too."

Vince breathed out an annoyed sigh. "Call a tow truck, bitch. Peace out." *Click.*

Dante just shook his head, not thinking much of it. Vince

was probably dealing with some Subway crisis like running low on tuna salad, so Dante decided to take the high road and cut the brother some slack for being a douche bag.

The only upside to this pain in the ass was that it happened *after* Dante's last swim lesson for the day. Sasha Edkins, the woman who owned and operated SafeSplash, had a zero-tolerance policy on bullshit. And her definition of the concept was broad, encompassing sickness, car trouble, family emergencies . . . basically everything but an employee's own death.

Dante glanced down at his blinging new watch and instantly felt like a tool. Here he was, wearing something on his wrist worth way more than the car he drove. He was freaking stranded. But the correct time was three minutes until two. Congratulations, ghetto fabulous dickhead.

Not expecting much, he rang Max as more of a test than anything else. Chances are the party boy would just laugh his ass off and then hang up.

One ring . . . two rings . . .

"Put down your hedge clippers, yard ape. We're going to the Shore Club," Max said right away. Who needed boring hellos in the age of caller ID?

Dante couldn't believe it. This guy had just called him a "yard ape"! It was one of the most offensive things anyone had ever said to him. Yet he found himself laughing anyway. "Man, one day you're going to say the wrong shit to the right person, and I hope I'm there to see you get your ass kicked."

Max cackled. "You know I don't mean anything by that shit, right? I'm just screwing with you."

"Yeah, I get that, man," Dante said.

"So you're not going to call the NAACP on my ass?"

"No, man, listen, I need a favor. My car just died, and I'm stuck on the causeway."

"That's an easy fix. Steal another one."

"Ha ha," Dante said, his irritation level rising, not toward Max necessarily but toward the whole freaking mess.

"Where are you?"

Dante glanced around, then called out an approximate location.

"Okay, I'm on my way," Max said. "But don't be standing on the side of the road with your shirt off. People might think I'm picking up a hustler."

"Stop being paranoid. Everybody already knows that you hire rent boys to come straight to your crib," Dante shot back. "Drive fast, homo. It's hot as shit out here."

He hung up and waited. It was hard work—the heat, the steam, the sun, the traffic. Fifteen minutes crawled by like an hour.

And then Max roared onto the shoulder in his Porsche, blasting North Pole A/C, jamming the Pussycat Dolls and Busta Rhymes, looking Rolex rich. He zipped down the passenger window and smiled like the smug little bastard he was. "Need a ride, sweetheart?"

Dante leaned down to meet him at eye level, grinning. "Go to hell."

"Get in. Girls in bikinis are waiting for us at the Shore Club. But first we have to swing by and pick up Pippa."

Dante looked over at his dead Honda. "What about my car, man? I need a ride to—"

"I'll help you with that later," Max cut in. "Nobody's going to mess with that piece of shit. It's fine where it is for now." One beat. "You might want to grab your fuzzy dice hanging from the rearview mirror, though. Just in case."

Dante hesitated, his mind running through the worst-case scenarios. What if his car got impounded? What if—

"Let's go!" Max yelled, revving the engine to punctuate his impatience.

Screw it. For the second time in the last hour, Dante went against his better instincts. He slipped into the front seat, instantly relishing the blast of cold air from the vent. "Damn, that feels good."

Max took off like a speed demon, singing along, "Don'tcha wish your girlfriend was a freak like me?"

Dante shook his head and leaned back, still trying to cool down.

Max snatched his Sidekick II from a slot in the dash and punched in a number. "Omar, it's Max. Check it out, a friend's car stalled on the causeway. Have it towed to the house and see what you can do with it . . . about a mile north of Bridge Road . . . uh, I don't know what make or model. It's a piece of shit . . ."

"Ninety-nine Honda Civic!" Dante hollered out.

"Did you get that? Okay. Thanks, Omar. You're awesome." Then Max signed off and muttered, "Worthless jizz monkey."

Dante laughed.

"He's supposed to take care of all our cars," Max started. "You know, keep them washed, waxed, gassed up, handle all the routine maintenance. Well, it—"

"Hold up," Dante interrupted. "Let me get this straight. You don't even put *gas* in your own car?"

Max answered with a diffident shrug. "That's what Omar's around for, man. Listen to what I'm trying to tell you. The dude's a slack ass who spends half the day jerking off to Internet porn. Look at the interior of this car. He didn't even wipe it down with Armor All last time."

Dante looked at him in disbelief. "You are one spoiled little pussy."

"We're just trying to give this loser a job and keep him off the streets," Max argued. "If it wasn't for my family, he'd probably be standing outside a school yard with a hard-on."

"What are you talking about?" Dante asked.

"The dude's a registered sex offender. I think they wrote Megan's Law just for him."

"For real?"

"No, I'm just talking shit," Max admitted. "But he could

be a pedophile. You never know about people." He punched the gas and left a BMW in his Porsche dust.

Suddenly, with no signal warning, a Cadillac Escalade land yacht switched lanes.

Dante experienced a quick life flash. He gripped the door handle, prayed that Max could maneuver as fast as he talked, and cursed himself for not wearing his seat belt.

"Aaaaaaaaaaaaagh," Max screamed. He seemed to do the defensive driving math in a nanosecond. Breaking hard would get them rammed by the Lexus following too close, so he made a sharp turn onto the shoulder at seventy miles per hour, just missing a dangerous sideswipe into the railing. Then he gave the machine all the juice it could handle, rocketing past the Cadillac by millimeters, at which point he jerked back onto the road, simultaneously cutting off the SUV and flipping his middle finger to the man at the wheel. *"Asshole!"*

Dante watched the action behind them unfold in his mirror, bracing himself for the demolition sound track of colliding metal. Brakes were slammed. Horns were honked. It came *thisclose* to a multicar pileup. But in the end, what developed was nothing more than a bunch of pissed-off drivers on a hot Miami afternoon, collectively hating the guts of whoever operated the Porsche with the BABY DON vanity plate.

Max unclenched his knuckles from the steering wheel and laughed a nasty laugh, mocking the fact that they'd just been as close to needing a helicopter ambulance as God to grace.

Finally, Dante allowed himself to breathe. "You're crazy, man." But even as the words tripped out of his mouth, he didn't know what the point of them was. Sharp criticism? Simple observation? Total awe? Or maybe a combination of all three.

Max twisted up the stereo volume and bobbed his head to Kanye West's "Gold Digger," drumming a white-boy rhythm on the wheel. "So what'd you do today?" he asked.

"Some of us have to *work*," Dante replied. "I had a swim lesson at seven o'clock this morning."

"How'd it go? Can you float on your back yet?"

Dante laughed.

"I got a blow job today," Max announced.

"Good for you," Dante said. He paused a beat. "I hope the guy knew what he was doing." And then he lost it, cracking himself up.

Max laughed, too. He raised his right index finger. "Okay, that was pretty good. Seriously, though, I've got this awesome scam going. I post ads for actresses on Craig's List and pretend I'm a production assistant casting for my dad's next movie."

Dante looked at him to put the guy talk in sharper focus. "You're screwing with me, right?"

"No," Max said. He was half smiling. But he was all the way insisting. "The girls show up, I have them run a few lines from an old script that's been passed on, and they always end up doing something slutty to help me remember them. And you know, there are some *very* talented aspiring actresses out there. I book a room at the Raleigh and do this a few times a week."

Dante shook his head, wondering what it must be like to exclusively live a life of fun, frat games, and fornication. "So, in other words, you're exploiting the dreams of naïve and desperate young girls."

Max considered the question. "Yes. And it's very important work."

Dante leaned back and laughed.

Max glanced over, and his gaze honed in on Dante's watch. "Whoa! Hold on a minute. Check out bling baby! What's up? Did you mug Bow Wow last night?"

Dante's heart beat a little faster with the adrenaline of embarrassment. "I'm earning it."

"You must also be teaching the lonely housewives how to swim after they put the kids down for a nap."

"It's not like that," Dante said. "Swimming's a big deal to parents. Why turn down a bonus?"

"Yeah, why do that?" Max replied, doing something funny with his eyebrows as he pulled off onto a side street, peeling around corners until he jerked to a stop in front of a sad-looking cottage. He turned to Dante. "Okay, ice queen, you'll have to fold yourself into a pretzel back there. Pippa's got great ta-tas, and I want them up front with me."

Dante jumped out to oblige, taking in the dilapidated Shangri-la with the Spanish tile roof that should've been replaced years ago. It made him feel less alone to know that he wasn't the only one in the group who couldn't burn cash like bonfire wood.

"Holy shit," Max sputtered.

A second later, Dante was thinking the same thing. Only he had the coolness to be silent about it.

Pippa's strut toward the car was the direct cause of paralyzed limbs, open-mouthed drool, and redirected blood flow. In a black diamante-studded Lycra bikini and pink sarong with beaded fringe, the girl was undressed just enough to make male lifeguards ignore drowning children. Her breasts pouted ambitiously against the thin material of her top, presenting the please-God-please possibility that there might be a luscious cargo spill.

"Just kill me now," Max groaned.

Dante waved hello and began negotiating his long body into the small space behind the front seats.

"Dante, no!" Pippa protested. "You're too big for the back." She giggled. "You'll crawl out with scoliosis. I'll squeeze in."

"Oh, he doesn't mind," Max said, shoving Dante into the tight spot with a firm hand. "If Anne Frank stayed in the attic that long, he can handle the ride to the Shore."

Pippa laughed and bounced inside to claim her seat, filling the tiny cabin with her delicious tropical scent, a heady mix of passion fruit, coconut, musk, and orange flower.

"You smell fantastic," Max said. "It makes me want to lick your—"

"It's Miami Glow by J. Lo," Pippa cut in, halting the obscene not a moment too soon. "And *you* won't be licking anything." One beat. "Except maybe your own wounds."

Dante laughed.

Max mouthed silent curses at him through the rearview mirror. "The stray in the back should feel *grateful* that I picked him up on the side of the road."

Pippa twisted around, a question in her eyes.

"My car broke down," Dante explained.

"Oh, no!" Pippa responded dramatically. "That sounds like Stress Central." She twisted a lock of hair around her finger. "I wish I *had* a car to break down. My mum says I should think about getting a job soon. I don't know what I'd do, though. I can't jump into a dodgy restaurant job. That'd be bloody awful. And I don't want to rot behind a counter ringing up things all day."

"I could get you an audition for my father's next movie," Max offered.

Pippa perked up. "Do you mean that?"

Dante laughed, slapping Max on the back of the head. "Don't listen to him. There's no part in his dad's movie."

Max smiled and checked his watch. "Okay, ladies, this should be an interesting lab test."

"What's that?" Pippa wondered.

"Hitting the Shore Club pool at three o'clock. You're usually shit out of luck on claiming a chair by ten. If Vanity can pull this off, then I'll ask for her autograph."

Dante's mind stopped. Until now, he had no idea that Vanity St. John was part of the day's equation.

"She's been so frosty to me ever since I got here," Pippa complained. "What did she say when you told her I was coming along?"

"Nothing," Max assured her. "She was cool with it."

"I just don't get it," Pippa went on. "I've tried so hard to be nice to her, but she still acts like a total bitch."

"Vanity's cool," Max insisted. "Shit, I've known her since the first grade. It just takes her a minute to warm up. That's all."

Pippa shrugged. For her, it seemed enough of an answer.

But Dante needed more to shake his weird feeling. Part of him wanted to hop out and catch a bus back home. The other part couldn't wait to see what would happen next.

From: Wilmar

Are you dressing up for Eric's Godchild party?

1:54 pm 6/23/05

chapter nine

Christina couldn't take her eyes off Vin Diesel.

Three very gorgeous and almost naked women were taking turns feeding the bald and buff superstar. Either he was ready for a Comedy Central spotlight, or they were just easily entertained. Because after his every turn of phrase, the trio of bimbo bunnies serenaded him with a chorus of animated giggles.

"Christina, it's not polite to stare," her mother mock scolded before tossing back a look to satisfy her own curiosity. "Who is that?"

"Vin Diesel," Christina whispered.

It was obvious that the name didn't register with Paulina Perez.

"The actor," Christina clarified.

"Never heard of him."

"You know, *The Fast and the Furious, XXX, The Pacifier.*"

"Have I seen those movies?"

"We *own* the DVDs."

Her mother shrugged. "Half the time I'm doing something else when the television's on. Too bad Tom Hanks didn't show up here today. Now there's an actor."

"You're such a Republican," Christina teased, taking in a heaping spoonful of zuppa del golfo, a rich tomato broth with mussels, squid, and other seafood.

"What's wrong with that?" Paulina asked archly.

"Nothing, Mom," Christina assured her, not wanting to get into it. After all, Paulina was trying to be nice. No reason to spoil her effort with a bad attitude.

Paulina smiled, breathing in the ocean, the air, and the sunshine. "I'm glad we did this, sweetie. It feels like we're really away from everything, doesn't it?"

Christina nodded. They were having lunch among the rich and famous, one of their semiregular mother-daughter outings. Today they decided to hit Ago, a restaurant owned by Robert DeNiro and nestled inside the Shore Club, a sprawling South Beach hotel property with room rates as high as fifteen thousand dollars a night.

Upon arrival they navigated the Shore Club's stark, all-white lobby, through a colorful garden walkway, past Skybar—one of the most exclusive nightspots in Miami—and finally into the oh-so-expensive Italian eatery, where they opted for seating on the rustic outdoor patio. They were lucky to secure a perfect table overlooking the water.

"Are there any gay kids at your school?" Paulina asked as she took a stab at her grilled salmon.

Instantly, Christina's body went hot with alarm. She lived in constant fear of someone—especially her mother—confronting her with questions about her sexuality. "What do you mean?"

Paulina gave her a curious glance. "Do you know of any gay students at MACPA?"

Once Christina realized that the inquiry had nothing to do with her personally, she relaxed a bit. Were there any gay students at the Miami Academy for Creative and Performing Arts? Hmm. As she considered this, she fought back a laugh. "MACPA *is* an arts school. There's, like, a musical theater department and everything."

"So the answer's yes?" Paulina said, not getting the absurdity at all.

"I don't have firsthand evidence," Christina went on. "But, yes, I think it's safe to assume that there are gay students at MACPA." She paused a beat. "Just like it'd be safe to assume that there are tennis fans at Wimbleton."

Paulina didn't pick up on the sarcasm. "I'm just asking because my political consultant was telling me about a high school in the city that held a separate gay prom last spring. Isn't that terrible?"

Christina looked at her mother probingly. "What's terrible

about it? That the school couldn't have just one prom or that they actually held a separate one?"

Paulina didn't hear the question. Or maybe she just chose not to answer it. "The line has got to be drawn somewhere. This reminds me of the same-sex marriage issue. It's one more tradition going down the drain. I also heard about a lesbian who won homecoming queen at a high school last year. She wore a *tuxedo* to the celebration! I just hate to see innocent, time-honored rituals openly mocked by these gays who have no respect for what's decent and normal."

These gays. Christina sought refuge in the Pellegrino sparkling water as the intolerant words ricocheted inside her mind. A passive-aggressive little fantasy began to take shape. What would her mother do if Christina made a coming-out announcement right here at Ago? Probably throw up all over Vin Diesel. Ha! The image of that amused her just enough to get through the uncomfortable moment.

Inside, Christina had to laugh. Humor was the only way to survive dealing with Paulina Perez. Because deep down, she knew that any attempt at open communication with her mother would backfire. In fact, Christina would probably end up shackled at Refuge, the religious-based youth program run by Love in Action International. Parents were sending their teenagers there for as long as six weeks. Basically, for two thousand dollars a week, campers got a prisonlike environment and went through a host of humiliating exercises to "de-gay" their natural orientations.

"Things are moving in a dangerous direction," Paulina continued. "Teenagers these days have a laid-back attitude about the destructive gay lifestyle. They go on experimental rampages and actually think it's cool. Experts say this can set them up for some serious issues down the road."

Christina wanted to walk away from the subject altogether, but she just couldn't resist. "Mom, you can find experts for the other side of the argument, too."

Paulina was visibly flummoxed by the rebuttal. Probably because she was so used to speaking to groups of people who thought exactly like her. "What other side is there?"

For a moment, Christina nervously played with her dark, choppy hair, shifted her floppy hat, adjusted her giant sunglasses, and glanced down at her scuffed cowboy boots. "Everybody knows that boys are supposed to be with girls and vice versa, but there's another way to be. And everybody knows that, too. I don't see anything wrong with challenging traditions, especially if a group of people is feeling left out. Think about it. Can you imagine the world today if black people hadn't fought against the system?"

Paulina shook her head and leaned forward to hiss, "I'm not going to sit here and allow you to equate the gay activist agenda with the civil rights movement. It's not the same thing. Being gay is a choice. And it's all about sex."

By this point, Christina didn't have the will nor the desire to turn away from the debate. "Says one *expert*. And maybe

Fred Phelps, that minister from Kansas. Do you really want to be on *his* side of the argument?"

Paulina didn't try to hide her annoyance. "Who's Fred Phelps?" she asked in a snappish tone.

"He stages antigay protests and runs a website—god-hatesfags-dot-com." Christina allowed a single beat to pass. "Oh, and I'm pretty sure he's Republican."

As Paulina leaned back in her chair, her eyes narrowed angrily. She was a near dead ringer for Latin icon Gloria Estefan—only dressed to grip-and-grin with the Conservative Women's Voters League in a smart navy suit and low heels. Pushing her half-eaten plate away, she sniffed, "He sounds like a gross extremist. And I've never claimed everyone in my party."

"I just don't understand why you get so worked up about these things," Christina said, working hard to adopt a diplomatic tone. "I mean, at the end of the day, who really cares? So what if two boys want to go to the prom together. If they're renting tuxes and buying boutonnieres and going out for a romantic dinner, then that's good for the economy, right? Small businesses benefit. Doesn't everybody win?"

"It's about *values,* Christina." Paulina shook her head. "You're too young to understand. Not to mention you're in this hippie chick / artist phase that makes you want to wrap your arms around the whole world. Well, just wait until you get married and have children of your own. The word 'Republican' won't sound so dirty to you then. In fact, you'll *embrace* it." She nodded smugly. "Trust me on that." After a knowing wink, she flagged down the waiter for a cup of coffee, then unleashed a heavy sigh. "You might not think these issues are important. But the voters will."

"Is that what your 'consultant' says?" Christina asked pointedly.

"Yes," Paulina said, her brown eyes brightening, as they always did whenever the subject of her political aspirations hit the table. "He thinks the family values front is a good place for me. It's a hot button topic, and, for middle-of-the-road voters, it's less polarizing to see a woman come down on the conservative side of things, which will serve me well once I begin my new campaign for stronger values in the schools."

All Christina could do was pray that MACPA was *not* on her mother's target list. "What kind of campaign?" she asked, more out of polite curiosity than anything else.

"I'm going to shut down school-sponsored gay-straight alliance clubs," her mother said matter-of-factly.

Christina's mouth dropped open in total shock. "You've *got* to be joking."

"I never joke about politics, sweetie." Paulina sipped gingerly at the coffee that had just swooped down. "Tell me, is there such a club at MACPA?"

Christina was shedding psychic blood now. It seemed so unbelievably cruel, that the woman who should be her biggest fan was her biggest enemy, even if it was in secret. For a single, guilty moment, she wondered why fate had claimed her father's life in that car accident, the same one that her mother had lived through. To wish the reverse was a morbid thought. But that didn't stop her from having it.

"Well, is there such a club?" Paulina repeated.

"Not that I know of," Christina answered, still trying to process this bizarre notion of her mother waging public war on gay teenagers . . . just like her. "I take it this brilliant consultant of yours isn't from Miami."

Paulina's eyebrows met in the middle. "Actually, he's based out of Washington. Why?"

"Because a guy from here would know better. People love Miami because they can be who they are." Christina believed what she was saying. But she wasn't living it. And the question that triggered was a simple one: When would she have the courage to start?

Paulina stared at Christina carefully, as if sensing obvious trouble ahead. Raising the issue of the consultant's competency had been marginally patronizing. And this was on top of the counterattack that painted her mother as either a dense homophobe or an advocate for human rights violations.

It was as if she was looking at Christina for the very first time and finally seeing a daughter who was more than the self-absorbed, moody artist who kept her head buried in silly Japanese comic books. Yes, she defied fashion laws with her forcefully unostentatious, walking-unmade-bed style. Yes, she emerged only periodically from her cocoon to engage in a friendship clique comprised mainly of Wilmar and Eric, two fantasy fan boys who wore their social outcast status like Purple Hearts.

But Christina could also challenge her mother with strong left-versus-right verbal volley. She thought things. She felt things. She could passionately articulate them, too. Where had this come from? The question was swimming in the eyes of Paulina Perez. So was the sobering realization that the fights about wearing ratty, crocheted shawls and developing an interest in dating boys had—practically over the course of one lunch—segued into conflicts much more complicated. And it was obvious that this wouldn't be the stuff of great mother-daughter bonding.

"He's one of the best," Paulina said finally, blindly defending her inside-the-beltway boy.

Christina glanced up, sensing a hum of awareness from the crowd. The source was Nicole Richie, the famous-for-being-famous star of *The Simple Life,* looking rail thin but radiant as she sashayed onto the patio and injected the area with a sudden, palpable celebrity energy.

"If he's so good, then he should know that an antigay crusade wouldn't work in Miami," Christina remarked. She waited for the not-so-subtle comment to detonate, and when it did, she caught a slight whiff of doubt coming from Paulina's side of the table.

Suddenly, another low rumble rose up from the Ago mini-mob. This time it was Vanity St. John, generating considerably more commotion than Nicole Richie had. Vanity wore a short, kaleidoscopic Pucci dress so wild, colorful, and revealing that it instantly confirmed her status as the center of the universe. At least this one at the Shore Club.

Christina tried to hide the fact that she needed to swallow. Instead, she took a deep breath, watching as Vin Diesel craned his bull neck to get an unobstructed view of the celebutante. The man who played Riddick was loudly ignoring his personal harem, and the expression on his face told the Ago flock that, given the chance, Vanity might be worth the risk of jail time.

There was a flush on Christina's face that had nothing to do with the heat. She stared intently, trying to keep her mouth shut, clocking Vanity's every move as the beautiful starlet smiled slyly in the bright sunlight and waved hello to Owen Wilson, the thirty-something actor who was way too old to be drooling over a high school girl.

Vanity flashed a look in Christina's direction and seemed visibly relieved to encounter a familiar face that wasn't openly calculating a plot to get her up to one of the rooms. She made a whiz-bang beeline for the table. "Hey, girl!" Vanity exclaimed, enveloping Christina in a quick hug.

After the necessary introduction to Paulina, Vanity perched down onto an empty chair and launched into a breathless tale without preamble. "This day is completely insane. I was supposed to meet my publicist here for lunch, and she just called to cancel. You won't believe this—Katee K was arrested."

Christina and her mother traded looks of mutual dismay.

Katee K was the breakout star of the Disney Channel series *Kamp Kool,* a harmless sitcom about the summer camp adventures of a well-meaning but troublesome teen, played to scenery-chewing effect by, of course, Katee K, the squeaky-clean marketing phenom who was ruling the airwaves with a hit single, "Some Girl Said," and invading Target stores with her own clothing line, room décor merchandise, and youth cosmetics. In short, the second coming of Hilary Duff was on a mission to conquer the world.

"For what?" Christina demanded to know. Granted, she was no Katee K fan, but the silly teen star was ubiquitous. *Everybody* knew who she was. And that included the culturally clueless Paulina.

"She stabbed her mother," Vanity said flatly. One beat. "Can you believe that?"

"Oh my God," Christina murmured.

"She's not dead," Vanity went on. "She's in stable condition. The doctors say she'll be fine. But Katee K's in police custody. I mean, this is attempted murder."

"How old is she?" Christina asked.

"Thirteen," Vanity replied. "My publicist reps her, too, and I've heard horror stories about this mother. Not that she deserves to be stabbed, but she uses Katee as the family meal ticket and works her like a mule. It's no wonder the girl snapped."

All of a sudden, Paulina stood up. "Why don't you girls sit here and gossip. Have a dessert—my treat. There's an event I was planning to skip today, but the responsibility is gnawing at me. I should put in a quick appearance." She shifted to address Vanity directly. "Could you give Christina a ride home?"

"Sure," Vanity said easily.

But Christina was mortified, feeling quite certain that right now Vanity St. John was wishing she'd never even said hello.

"Perfect. I'll see you at home tonight, sweetie." And then Paulina was gone, offering a buoyant, "Have fun, girls!" before disappearing from the patio.

Initially, there was an awkward silence.

"You don't have to take me home," Christina said apologetically, desperately trying to fill it. "I can catch a cab or call my friend Wilmar. I mean, I'm sure you have other plans."

"Actually, I don't," Vanity said. "Katee K stabbed them to death, remember?" She smiled.

Christina was suspended over the abyss, fighting with superhuman effort the overwhelming impulse to jump up and down. One-on-one time with Vanity St. John? It seemed too good to be true.

"Besides," Vanity went on, "this will be good homework for me. By direct order from my therapist, I need to make a girlfriend or two."

Christina looked at her curiously, waiting for the punch line. But it never came. "You're not kidding, are you?"

Vanity shook her head.

"I thought you had all the friends in the world."

"I have all the *acquaintances* in the world," Vanity corrected. "And on Saturday night, there's a big difference between the two."

This confession intrigued Christina. There was something about Vanity that added up to so much more than her beauty, her fame, and her wealth. "I've never been to a therapist before. What's it like?"

"Intense," Vanity said. "If you do it right. Some people just skim the surface and talk about the time somebody stole their bicycle. I've been going once a week for six months. I'll probably be on the couch for years." She sighed. "Just so you know, I'm totally screwed-up. You might want to catch that cab after all."

Christina smiled. It seemed incredible that Vanity could just drop her defenses and announce information like that to someone she barely knew. "I *should* be in therapy," Christina offered. Yes, it was lame. But in terms of surrendering inhibitions, this was heavy duty for her.

"So you're an emotional mess, too?" Vanity asked lightly.

"You have no idea," Christina assured her.

"Well, at least we're not stabbing people. Katee K trumps both of us, don't you think?"

Christina laughed.

Vanity laughed, too.

"Do you want to share a dessert?" Christina asked. "I can't finish one by myself."

"Oh, I never eat dessert," Vanity said. "I save my calories for alcohol."

Christina experienced a hot flash of pure embarrassment. If ever there was a moment when she felt seventeen years old going on twelve, then this was it. *Do you want to share a dessert?* Ugh! Resisting an urge to vault over the ledge and bury herself in the sand, she said, "I'll skip it, too."

Vanity peered up at the blazing sun. "It's a gorgeous day. We should hang out by the pool."

"Can we do that?" Christina wondered aloud. "I thought you had to be a hotel guest."

Vanity waved off the concern. "I have VIP status here. It's cool."

Christina glanced down at her bohemian ensemble. "It sounds like fun, but I don't have a swimsuit."

"No problem. We'll find one for you at the boutique," Vanity suggested.

Christina felt an instant wave of panic. Swimwear at the Shore Club would be top designer only and easily run at least two hundred dollars.

"And don't worry about the price," Vanity chimed in, as if reading her mind. "I've got house credit for days from doing promo appearances here. It's on me." She stood up. "Ready?"

Christina nodded, careful to mute her enthusiasm and excitement. Only if she played things as cool as Vanity St. John could she survive this day. And the pressure to do just that made her shiver in the ninety-degree heat.

With a shake of her swan's neck, Vanity led the way, and her mere movement created a look-now stir among the Ago herd. Certain male eyes were rheumy with kill-me-now lust; most female ones were jungle green with I-give-up jealousy. But Vanity just marched on, like a messenger goddess from a superior civilization who walked on the water of her own liquid charisma.

Christina trailed behind her. In a matter of minutes, her dull life had been steamed up in ways she hadn't counted on today. Down deep in her beat-up Chloe bag, her Sidekick II jingle-jangled. She peeked at the screen, saw a text from Wilmar, and felt a frisson of guilt. Why? Because she felt no inclination to even skim the message.

She knew what the deal was. It would be endless questions about Eric's *Godchild* party, celebrating the *manga* by Kaori Yuki. Everyone was expected to bake a homemade tea cake and arrive in costume as their favorite *Alice in Wonderland* character. Several days ago it sounded like great fun. In fact, the event had been looming out to Christina as a social lifeline.

But now alternatives were beginning to present themselves. Max had sought out her company the other night. Vanity was seeking it out now. The clichéd fork in the road was right in front of her. One path led her back to the socially inferior outcasts she knew; the other could take her to exciting new places . . . and perhaps even embolden her to start living in the hot danger of reality as opposed to the mild safety of fantasy.

"Aren't you going to answer that?" Vanity asked.

The choice was first grade simple. "No, I'll get it later," Christina said.

From: Mimi

Forgive me 4 lunch! Who knew Katee K would
turn into Jason from Fri the 13th?? Heard
from InStyle. Shoot is set for next month.
MAJOR photographer.

3:13 pm 6/23/05

chapter ten

"**A**bsolutely not," Vanity said, shooing away the one-piece bathing suit.

"But I can't wear a bikini," Christina protested. Miserably, she glanced down at her chest. "I'm too flat."

Vanity rolled her eyes. "Don't be stupid. Flat is good. *Models* are flat. The *Playboy* look is so over. Have you met Max's sister, Shoshanna?"

Christina nodded as she browsed another rack in the tiny boutique. "Yes, I met her *and* her boobs."

Vanity giggled. "You're so funny. But you're so right, too. It's like, 'Hi, I'm Shoshanna, and these are my tits.' *So* ridiculous. And it's not even that attractive. I mean, I'm sure most guys would disagree with me, but let's face it, most guys are gross. Look at you. I would *kill* to be that skinny. You're every designer's dream. Couture was made for your body. I know you've got this whole bohemian thing going, which is cool, but you should keep an eye out for some vintage couture when you're out there digging for finds. It'd look great on you."

"Thanks," Christina murmured shyly. For a moment, she fixed a penetrating stare on Vanity. "I really wouldn't know what to hunt for, though." There was an awkward pause. "Maybe we could go together sometime."

"Sure," Vanity chirped. "That'd be fun." She snatched a mango-colored tankini and pushed it into Christina's hands. "This'll be perfect. Try it on."

Christina stared doubtfully at the single-strap, form-fitting tank and boy shorts set.

"Trust me," Vanity insisted. "You'll be *delicious.*" She clapped her hands. "Now hurry up. We have to be at the pool by the time Max and Pippa get here. Otherwise, she'll try to get in on this and have me foot the bill for her entire fall wardrobe."

Christina ducked behind a curtain into a narrow dressing room. "What do you mean by that?"

Vanity vented while Christina gave the tankini a whirl. "She never has any money. I mean, *never.* So you end up paying for everything. Classic example: It was her idea to go shopping the other day, but—surprise, surprise—she was completely broke. Her plan was to take back old stuff for refunds and then buy something new. How disgusting is that?

Anyway, I would've been asked to pick up the difference on some outfit that barely fit her. *And* pay for her Starbucks fix. *And* the check, had we gone to a restaurant. *And* her movie ticket, had we done that."

"Do you think she's using you to buy her things?" Christina asked.

"No, because it's not just me. She does it to everybody. If Pippa was standing here right now, she'd hit you up for the money to get a Diet Coke. I swear. It's ridiculous. And it bugs the shit out of me. If I'm going to sponsor the daily living expenses for a charity case, then it's going to be a poor child in Africa. Okay? Not Pippa Keith. I mean, quit bitching about your stupid allowance and get a job already. You know?"

Christina said nothing.

"How are you doing in there?" Vanity asked.

"I'm not sure," Christina murmured.

Vanity flung open the flimsy curtain. "Silly bitch. You look *amazing*."

Christina stood there modestly, one hand on the bare skin where the tank top stopped just short of her belly button, the other hand on the left hem of the boy shorts that barely covered her butt cheek.

"Where did you get an ass like that?" Vanity asked.

Christina stared back at her in shock.

"Oh, I forgot," Vanity said quickly. "You're a Latin girl." She zeroed in on the glorious Perez bottom. "But it's not that big. It's, like, *perfect*. God, you make me sick."

Christina glanced at the price. Instantly, her eyes widened. "This is three hundred dollars!"

Vanity waved off the money concern and carefully removed the tag. "They're all about that much. It's no big deal. Wear it straight to the pool."

"But it'll take me forever to pay you back," Christina whispered.

"Would you stop!" Vanity insisted. "You're not paying me back. This is just one of the perks I get. It's not costing me a dime. I'm happy to share."

"Well . . . thank you," Christina gushed quietly. "Still, I feel like I should offer you *something*."

Vanity glanced down at the sketchbook that Christina took with her everywhere. All of a sudden, a crazy idea came to mind. "Draw my picture. A comic book version of me. Turn me into a superheroine. You know, like Batgirl or Supergirl."

Christina beamed. "Okay!" Then she dove for her pad, flipped it to a blank page, and started skating her pencil across the paper in a series of long, sweeping, rapid-fire strokes. "Stand right there," she demanded.

Vanity laughed. "I didn't mean right now!"

"Just give me a minute," Christina said, her intensity total, her left hand sketching furiously. "This is just a rough concept. I'm trying to get your overall shape and profile. Don't mind me. Keep talking."

For some reason, being an artist's subject made Vanity feel

more vulnerable than being a photographer's. "Do you want to hear something completely crazy?" Vanity asked.

"What?" Christina wondered, barely looking up, her eyes alternating from Vanity's body to the pad.

"I got a call from my publicist. *InStyle* wants to do a story on what's in my purse. Of course, it won't be about what's really in there. They don't want to know about the dirty thong underwear that's stuffed in the side pocket or the pack of American Spirits that's unopened because the last thing I need to start is another bad, self-destructive habit. The list of contents will be carefully engineered. It'll be cutting-edge stuff that's not in there now, but that I'll get for free for saying that it was. Like a new lipstick with an insane name like Orgy. So, ultimately, the article about *my* purse will have almost nothing to do with me."

Christina's pencil stopped moving. "How bizarre."

"Welcome to my life," Vanity said. "That's what being famous is all about."

"Do you like it?" Christina asked.

"Right now I'd have to say no. But if you ask me again in five minutes, when we go out to the pool and instantly get all the chairs we need at peak sun time, then I'd have to tell you yes."

Christina gave her one of those long, intense stares, then turned over the sketch pad for Vanity's inspection.

Vanity gasped. The instant drawing looked exactly like her—the hair, the eyes, the bridge of the nose, the mouth, every feature practically photo-exact. "Oh my God. This is amazing." For a long second, she just stared at Christina, envying her for possessing such a talent. It made Vanity wonder what she could do besides make paparazzi move like rats in a cage.

Her Sidekick II jingled.

Vanity saw that it was Max and picked up right away. "Hey, where are you?"

"On the way. I was thinking all the girls could sunbathe topless. That way you won't have to worry about tan lines."

Vanity rolled her eyes. "Oh, how thoughtful. And I suppose that idea has nothing to do with the fact that you're a complete sex maniac."

"Me?" Max asked with faux innocence. "I'm saving myself for marriage."

"By the time *you* get married, the only thing left will be . . . well, it's probably such a deviant act that nobody's thought to categorize it yet."

Max laughed. "Listen, just throw your superstar weight around and score us some chairs. We need five."

"Who's the fifth one for?" Vanity asked.

"Dante," Max said.

Vanity's stomach dropped. Maybe she did have talent after all. If she could get through the day acting like she didn't give a damn about Dante Medina, then she was a shoo-in for Best Actress in a Poolside Drama.

•   •   •

The Skybar pool at the Shore Club was sun worship to the nth degree. Total hard core. Burly bouncers muscled out club trash. Friendly cabana boys fetched twelve-dollar bottled waters. And at peak hours, the impression lingered that deck furniture could be more valuable than oceanfront property.

Apparently, Vanity had scored fame's top afternoon trick in South Beach—commandeering coveted pool chairs. Five chaise lounges were fanned out in a prime location, and she was pole positioned dead center, slaying the daytime crowd in a copper shell bikini top and thong bottom. She took one glance at Dante and looked up at the sun.

Max played social maestro and introduced Dante to Christina. "This girl's the only talented one among us going to MACPA," he said. "She's a real artist. The rest of us are hacks."

Christina smiled as the symmetrical cut of her hair dipped several long strands into her shy, secretive eyes.

"I'm not a hack!" Pippa protested with good humor. "When it comes to dancing, I know my onions."

Max stretched out on a chaise, closed his eyes, and tilted his face toward heaven. "You don't need school for dancing. Japanese tourists don't mind if you're a little clumsy as long as you're naked."

Everybody howled.

Vanity tilted up her stone-cold-fox body to check an incoming text message. She laughed and tapped out a quick reply. "Mimi's catching pure hell trying to deal with this Katee K situation."

"What could be worse than her singing or acting?" Max asked.

"You don't know?" Vanity delivered the question in that tone girls employ when they can't *wait* to tell. "She's in jail for stabbing her mother."

Pippa lurched forward. "Bollocks!"

Vanity nodded dramatically. "I'm totally serious."

"Have you heard that song of hers that's a hit?" Max asked. "The little bitch should've stabbed herself."

Dante chuckled and shook his head, sharing a secret smile with Vanity in the process.

"It's just so eerie," Christina put in. "I never would've imagined that Katee K could so much as step on a bug. She's so sugary sweet."

"A hundred bucks says she'll be doing porn by the time she's eighteen," Max said.

And that's what they did for the remainder of the afternoon.

Laughed.

Drank.

Shouted.

And hung out.

Dante held court on the far end of the chair arrangement. With Christina sitting between him and Vanity, he felt almost bulletproof, the slight distance providing thick protection for the weaker parts of his psyche. Vanity St. John could be dangerous. Compared to her, an expensive gift from a hopeful *Queer Eye* husband and an abandoned car were child's play.

A girl like her with a father like Simon St. John could cause real havoc in Dante's life. He knew this with rock-solid certainty. So he coached himself to stay strong, to stay focused, and most importantly, to stay away. But even as he ran his mind through the rules of discipline, he found his body reacting in ways that guaranteed those rules would one day be broken.

"God, these drinks are going right through me," Vanity announced to no one in particular. Suddenly, she was up and gliding panther quick across the deck, her perfect drum-tight buttocks grinding like a pepper mill. The tiny material of her thong was buried deep in the cleft of her ass, which, as far as Dante was concerned, made it the luckiest fabric in the world.

He felt a rise where it mattered. Slipping off his watch, he made the quick decision to leap into the pool before anyone could notice the tent forming in his board shorts. The water wasn't nearly cold enough. Still, it managed to hide the obvious. Dante swam under, finding it difficult to navigate through the crowd of bodies. When he came up, he overheard a conversation in full momentum.

"Did you see Vanity St. John? She looks so much better in real life," a model-perfect girl said. "I saw her in the last *Teen Vogue,* and they had her in this skanky outfit."

"A buddy of mine saw her at a party the other night," a guy put in. "He said she got wasted and hooked up with some stoner."

"I don't know what the big deal is," another girl said, far less attractive than the first. "I mean, what does she do besides look great in clothes? And you can't even say that she's a real model."

"Did you see the way the hotel people scrambled to get her chairs?" the guy asked. "Shit, I wish it was that easy for us. We've been hanging out here for four hours and can't get near one. That bitch crooks a finger and lands *five.*"

"I know," Girl Number One agreed. "I say we get drunk, and try to forget that we're not part of 'the Fabulous Five.'"

Dante stepped out of the pool and headed back to the group, drying off quickly with a towel and returning his watch to the naked wrist that missed it. "Guess what? We're topic A around here."

Pippa rose up first. "Really? What's the goss?"

Dante grinned. "They're calling us 'the Fabulous Five,'" he said. It didn't matter that he was basking in the reflected glory of Vanity's fame. The truth was, less than a year ago he was a greasy nobody, lifting heavy trays at a barbeque joint and going through the motions at a bottom-ranked public school.

But things were different now. He had a real chance at MACPA, a better job, some wild new friends, a serious piece of bling, and a plan to make his ultimate dream come true. Oh, yes. This would be Dante Medina's year.

And it was just getting started.

From: Dante

Can't make the game, man. Sorry. Got some
studio time. Peace.

9:03 pm 7/15/05

chapter eleven

Only homos wax," Breck Hopkins said, a Corona Light in one hand and a bottle of Ciroc vodka in the other. The easygoing Phi Delt sophomore from the University of Miami glanced up to wink at Shoshanna. "What do you think, baby girl?"

Lazily, she stretched her arms overhead, all the better to show off her new breasts, which were natural-looking teardrop implants courtesy of one of Miami's top plastic surgeons. Yes, before she could legally drive, Shoshanna had been given a license to make grown men cry. "I like guys with body hair. I think it's sexy."

Breck flicked up his Dave Matthews Band T-shirt to give her a flash of his furry chest.

Shoshanna giggled, snatching Breck's Mexican beer and

taking a generous swig, slithering her tongue down into the bottle neck to get a taste of the lime wedge stuffed inside.

Max wanted to rip out the fraternity boy's heart. It had something to do with his sister. It had something to do with the poker game, too. And if he hated his opponents, then he usually cleaned them out.

Tonight was frustrating as hell. The stakes were too low. A minimum three hundred-dollar buy-in? That was for pussies. Max wanted to see the look in a player's eyes when he not only realized that he couldn't come out on top, but when he knew that the loss would be unbearable. To watch someone crumble like that right before his eyes was more beautiful than a South Beach sunset.

"Lots of dudes wax," J.J. put in. He grabbed Breck's Ciroc and turned it upside down, like a homeless drunk underneath a bridge. The only thing missing was the brown paper bag.

"Duuuuude," Breck protested, "I'm trying to get my drunk on here. Chill."

"Oh, is that it?" J.J. challenged, pushing the vodka to Breck's side of the table. "I thought you were trying to do this." He nodded to Shoshanna and made the international squeezing tits gesture with his hands.

Breck grinned and hooked an arm around the girl's waist, slyly slipping a few fingers under the waistband of her too-tight Shagg Downtown jeans by Sally Hershberger. "Just doing my thing, bro. This is my good luck charm. Isn't that right, baby girl?"

In answer, Shoshanna made a dirty little show out of lighting a thirty-dollar stogie and putting it between her pink, pouty, heavily glossed lips.

"There's nothing hotter than a girl who knows how to smoke a cigar," Breck praised. And then his roaming hand took possession of Shoshanna's ass and squeezed. "I might need to fold, boys. I think there's a better pot right here."

Shoshanna beamed. This kind of attention was especially sustaining for the precocious girl. It made her feel beautiful, rebellious, special, and loved.

Max knew exactly where his sister was heading. By next summer, Joe Francis would probably have footage of her pulling up her top and showering with a girlfriend for his *Girls Gone Wild* video series. It seemed impossible to stop the runaway train that was Shoshanna Biaggi. Fast-forwarding to the girl at sixteen hardly required an active imagination. One rowdy spring break trip to Panama City Beach. One wild night at Harpoon Harry's. Endless shots of her blurred nude body on late-night infomercials.

And what could a brother do with a sister who looked like Shoshanna? Especially if that sister was desperate for attention and purging demons caused by an abandoning mother, an absent father, and an ambivalent stepmother/stepmonster. Well, shit. There was no chance of convincing a girl like that to pinky swear with the God Squad and join the True Love Waits virgin club at school. Of that Max was damn sure. So all he could do was keep an eye out for her and make certain that she partied safely. Or at least reasonably so.

J.J. ran a hand down his baby smooth arm. "I have to keep my body waxed for work."

Max gave him a look. "Oh, yeah? I didn't realize that Sears had such high grooming standards for their catalog models."

Breck and Shoshanna busted out into gusts of head-shaking, hysterical laughter.

The flush of humiliation was high and red on J.J.'s sculpted cheekbones. It took him several long seconds to recover, or maybe that's the time it required to download his snappy retort, "You suck, dude." And for him, this constituted heavy-duty debate.

Max cackled at the male model's ego meltdown. The fake crotch bulge fame of the Hilfiger tighty-whitey campaign had faded long ago. And months were like dog years in the demimonde of modeling, which, theoretically, made Jayson "J.J." James about . . . oh, thirty-five. So why was this middle-aged loser playing poker with high school and college kids? Instead, he should be reading sappy Mitch Albom books and waiting for his Levitra to kick in.

"Hey, what happened to that J. Crew thing you were supposed to do a few weeks back?" Max asked.

J.J. reached for Breck's Ciroc again. "That gig fell through, man. It was a location shoot at the CEO's crib in

Water Mill, and they decided to use Hamptons locals. Pissed me off."

But Max already knew about the J. Crew career waterloo. He also knew that J.J. had gone psycho bitch on his booker over it and been subsequently canned by his agency. Now he went around bragging that he was a "free agent." Happy talk for a has-been mannequin with anger management issues who couldn't find decent representation.

"Whatever," J.J. said. And then he drank deep on the grape-infused vodka. "Anyway, waxing isn't a fag thing. Lots of guys do it."

Breck shook his head, disagreeing with both J.J. and, quite possibly, the cards in his hand, too. He rocked back and forth to the crunching guitars of Weezer's "Beverly Hills" and peeked at *The Shawshank Redemption* DVD running silently on the plasma screen.

"I enjoy a good wax," Max admitted, bored with J.J. and ready to verbally abuse another jackass.

"Duuuuude," Breck sang. He searched Max's face for the punch line, and when it didn't drop, he said, "Seriously, bro?"

Max nodded. "I even get my junk waxed."

J.J. laughed and raised a hand for some dap. "Been there, dude."

Grinning, Max went through the stupid male-bonding ritual.

Breck dropped a hand onto his crotch. The worried look on his face said that a newscaster might've just reported that all the beer in the world had mysteriously disappeared. "Down here? No way. You're shitting me."

Max nodded again. "Chicks love it. You get better and longer blow jobs, not to mention lots of attention to the family jewels." He laughed a little. "I bet you'd have to give a girl your cat's hairball medicine if she went anywhere near your nut sack."

This brought down the house in the Biaggi party basement. As the belly laughs commenced, all elbows left the cash-green felt of the poker table. Had Max been a comedian with a first-time shot on Letterman, he would've *destroyed.*

The truth was, Max loved making people crack up. As far back as elementary school, he'd rise from his chair if the inspiration hit, recite monologues from Jay Leno, and get wall-to-wall laughs. Sometimes he thought about a career in comedy. But he knew how brutal the world of stand-up could be. It was that way for poor whack job nobodies from New Jersey. So for the rich son of a Hollywood action star? Shit. It'd be acts of psychological terrorism every day. Besides, Max didn't have the soul-deep compulsion to perform. He just liked to screw around with people. And he was good at it.

Tears were spilling out of Breck's eyes. "I'm fading, dude. I'm fading," he managed in between guffaws. "Man, I gotta take that one back to my boys at the house. That was some funny shit." He reached for Shoshanna again and edged her closer. "Ready for some real fun, baby girl?"

J.J. laughed, looking at Max as he did so.

Max grinned at Breck. But it was the reassuring smile of a serial killer with a bloody butcher knife. The drunk asshole had gone too far.

Shoshanna took advantage of the *High Noon* moment and stole more Corona.

Max stirred up some nervous energy by riffling his chips ambidextrously. The move made one thing crystal clear: He'd spent *hours* playing cards—real poker with real players. Max was a true backroom rock-n-roll gambler. Breck and J.J. were pretenders who'd learned how to fake their way through on the Internet. Big difference. Bigger consequences.

Before the last flop, Max had thrown down a medium pair of eights to get more money on the table. At this moment, he was fighting the urge to laugh in Breck's frat boy face. Right now Joe College actually thought he might be holding a strong hand. Max knew this because the guy's nipples were visibly hardening against the fabric of his snug shirt. It was a good tell that always had the asshole on a permanent losing streak. So when Max flipped over and revealed a pair of kings, he raked in everything.

Game on.

Game over.

Game out.

Breck tossed his best cards—two queens. Close. Very close. Just not close enough. "That's it for me, dude. I'm wiped clean."

"Me, too," J.J. said, turning a pair of red tens.

Max checked the time on his Sidekick. "It's still early, boys. What is this—a sewing circle?"

"Too rich for my blood," Breck grumbled. And then he stood up, grabbed his Ciroc, and reached for Shoshanna's hand. As he pulled her up the stairs, he turned back to give Max a significant look, rubbing it in that the night wouldn't be a total loss.

"Hold up, Sho," Max called. "I need to talk to you for a second."

Reluctantly, she relinquished Breck's hand and started down the steps, her body language talking major irritation. "What, Max?" she huffed.

"That guy's a tool," he whispered conspiratorially. "Why don't you hang out with me tonight?"

"I think he's hot," Shoshanna argued. "Besides, I like older guys. Boys my age are boring."

Max shook his head. "Compared to those stockbrokers at the sushi joint, I suppose Breck *is* your age. But he's a frat, Sho. And a frat's mind is stuck on—"

Shoshanna cut him off midsentence. "Chill. I won't do anything that you didn't have fifteen-year-old girls doing to you." She smiled.

He didn't smile back. "That's hardly a comfort."

"I didn't think it would be. But look at it this way—even at nineteen, Breck probably doesn't know half the things you knew at fifteen." And then she was gone.

Helplessly, Max watched them disappear. There were no options here. Sure, he could kick Breck's ass and throw him out. But then Shoshanna would get pissed off and take her revenge by doing something worse. If it wasn't this guy in the safety of their home, then it'd just be another one someplace more precarious. Hence, Max's open-door policy. No hassles, no judgment. Not the easiest path to take, but it kept his sister close to him, and they had to stick together because they only had each other to count on. Of course, Max blamed his idiot father for the way Shoshanna acted out. After all, you couldn't buy a girl new boobs for her fifteenth birthday and then expect her to spend her time at the mall.

J.J. lit up a fatty and headed over to the sofa to get good and baked. "Heard from Vanity lately?" he asked, stretching out and dragging deep. "I've been trying her for the last few weeks, and she won't return my calls."

"She's around," Max said. "How many times have you called? Maybe she thinks you're a stalker."

J.J. held out the hellacious herb as a silent offer to partake.

Max waved him off. He had enough vices—drinking, gambling, partying, scamming girls for commitment-free sex, being a lazy son of a bitch. Besides, he knew his ways. Poker had become its own kind of drug. And he was an addict. If he added marijuana to the mix, then he'd no doubt go tripping off into cocaine and meth and end up in rehab before turning eighteen. Paging Jack and Kelly Osbourne.

"Are you a businessman, Max?" J.J. asked.

Max poured a shot of 1800 tequila and sauntered over to the suddenly existential out-of-work model.

"Because I need a businessman," J.J. went on. His tone was serious. His eyes were almost gone. "They call you Baby Don. After Donald Trump, right? Are you that good?"

"You're high, man," Max laughed.

"I'm drunk, too. But I do my best thinking this way."

"Well, that explains a lot."

J.J. took another hit. "Seriously, man. I'm sitting on a major marketing opportunity."

"Right now you're sitting on your ass." Max knocked back his shot, closing his eyes until the liquor burned all the way down. "And it's an ass that even J. Crew didn't want."

J.J.'s mouth curled into a blissful smile as he shook his head. "I'm not talking shit, man. See . . . you're talking shit. Me . . . I'm trying to keep it real. You know what I'm saying?"

Max grinned. "That must be some damn good weed."

"Oh, it is, man . . . it is." J.J. stared up at the ceiling for several long portentous seconds. "But it's not half as good as this business deal that I'm talking about."

"Okay, I'm officially curious," Max admitted. "What is it?"

"I can't say . . . not yet."

"Screw you," Max snapped. "You're wasting my time." He walked away from the stoner to pour another shot. So this was his Friday night? Waiting around for Breck and Shoshanna to finish hooking up and listening to this pothead's crazy rant about making the next *Fast Money* cover.

"Friends or business," J.J. murmured. "Which one comes first for you?" He sounded vacant, but the question actually had some depth.

Max sipped slowly and thought about it. "That depends."

"On what?"

"How good the friend and how good the business." He drained the rest of the drink and made a quick decision to hit Prive, the massive club with a higher hot-girl quotient than the Playboy Mansion. Nightlife queen and Madonna-ex Ingrid Casares had put it on the map. Door patrol was fierce. To get in, a guy should be rolling with at least two drop-dead beauties. But for Max, his own smoking looks and the last name Biaggi were enough. It'd be open sesame to the VIP lounge, to the drinks, to the pretty girls. Like always.

Meanwhile, J.J. continued to venture. "So if the business potential was strong enough . . ."

"Then, yeah, I'd rethink the friendship," Max said impatiently. "Look, man, I'm sick of talking in circles. If you've got a deal you want me to consider, then bring it on. You know where to find me. Otherwise, I'm out of here. You're free to crash, but don't crap on the rug, okay?"

With that, Max grabbed his Sidekick and raced up the

stairs, into the sunroom, and directly onto the pool deck. What he saw next made the tequila rumble inside his stomach.

At the shallow end of the pool, Breck was stretched out with his pants unbuttoned, finger-combing Shoshanna's hair like Vidal Sassoon while she eagerly kissed her way down his stomach. "Yeah, baby girl," he moaned thickly. "That's it. Go south. You know what to do."

Max fled the scene, trying to erase the disturbing memory from his mind as he rushed into the house and headed upstairs to change clothes. With a rising anxiety to be someplace else, *anyplace else,* he quickly tossed on top-level club gear—a Robert Graham button-up Oxford with contrasting placket and undercuffs, Da'Mage jeans, and Gucci motorcycle boots.

On the way out, he encountered his stepmonster at the bottom of the stairs. She lingered there, swaying back and forth, balancing a fresh martini in her hand, obviously not her first one of the night.

"Going out?" Faith Biaggi, spouse number two of the trophy wife variety, unleashed those words with a hostility that must've been building up for hours.

"Yeah," Max said. He didn't have much to do with her. She didn't have much to do with him. As far as he was concerned, monosyllabic answers were conversations that went on too long.

"Well, if you happen to see your father out there tonight,

do me a little favor and tell him to go straight to hell!"

"No problem," Max said. "That's my message for the son of a bitch, too."

And then he dashed out of the house, made a beeline for the garage, and forced himself to look away from any lewd acts happening at the pool.

All of a sudden, a vicious plot came to mind. He doubled back to the driveway and body slammed Breck's Jeep, setting off the motion alarm, then slipped quietly into the garage, laughing as he heard Breck muttering curses and struggling to fasten his pants over his erection. Idiot jizz bag.

Of course, there might be one good thing about Shoshanna's X-rated antics. The pool boy didn't show up until Monday, which meant their father would be taking his early morning swim with Breck's DNA contaminating the water.

This brought a smile to Max's lips as he hopped into his Porsche, turned over the key, and revved the engine. Impulsively, he thought about calling Pippa. Maybe she wanted to join him for this impromptu clubland adventure. Deciding that he needed a few good laughs that only a wild girl like Pippa could provide, he activated speed dial.

No answer. Then voicemail.

Feeling a pang of loneliness settle in, he tried Vanity.

Same shit.

"Screw it," Max muttered, pushing away the sudden melancholy.

He'd go alone.

He'd get drunk.

He'd get laid.

And then he'd sleep until noon and start the whole thing over again tomorrow. Isn't that what the little redheaded bitch Annie loved to sing about?

The sun'll come out tomorrow . . .

From: R. Kelley

STILL waiting 4 your night visit.

5:11 pm 7/23/05

chapter twelve

Vanessa Medina dropped down the dish of tamales, egg surprise, and chorizo with a loud *thwack*. It landed on the table like a cluster bomb. The gooey scrambled casserole slurped about. A hunk of the Mexican pork sausage slid onto the table. Amazingly, most of the food was still there to eat.

Dante looked at his mother, emptied some hot sauce onto the plate, and started shoveling it in.

"You want something to drink?" Her Spanish accent was thick, clipped, and seething with oppressed anger.

"Coke," he answered, his mouth full.

A few seconds later the soda can crashed in front of him. *Bam.*

"Thank you." His tone was sunnier than the moment called for, and in the Medina household, even the slightest hint of sarcasm was considered full-scale mouthing off.

Vanessa shot him a glare, stomping out of the kitchen and into the living room of their two-bedroom apartment. She stacked a few pillows onto the ottoman to elevate her feet, eased into her battered recliner, and clicked on a tape of the previous week's *Amor Descarado,* her favorite soap opera on Telemundo.

As son and man of the house, Dante was acutely sensitized to his mother's revolving moods. Tonight she was pissed off. Yesterday, she'd been the same way. Ditto the day before that. He tried to pinpoint the possible reasons why, then gave up. Silence had always been her preferred smoke screen. When she felt ready to talk, conflicts would get resolved. No sooner. No later.

Dante wolfed down his favorite dishes, guzzled the Classic Coke, and indulged himself with a loud, disgusting belch that felt fantastic after the heavy meal. "Excuse me," he murmured.

"Pig," Vanessa grunted.

Dante grinned. That kind of acknowledgment was potentially a good sign. Any minute now she might decide to vent her issues with him. But then again the silent treatment could stretch on for days.

Their relationship was claustrophobic—close living quarters, unspoken grief about her husband and his father, the inevitable mutual emotional dependency that went along with that, and the disconnect of him wanting a better life and her being passively, some psychiatrists might say depressively, content with the one that seemed to provide her little happiness.

Dante's cellular chimed to the ringtone of Pretty Ricky's "Grind with Me." He saw MAX CALLING and picked up right away, needing to lighten the mood that was too heavy for a Saturday night. "Hey, man."

"What's up, Snoop Dogg? Let's get wasted."

Dante smiled. It sounded like the perfect medicine. "You don't have to twist my arm."

"How does Mansion sound?"

"Never been, but I'm game."

"Oh, man, you'll shit when you see this place. It's one of those multilevel city block clubs that could cram in three thousand people but is still choosy at the door. Real Gothic vibe. And the girls are freaking unbelievable. If a bitch is half-dressed at Mansion, she might as well call herself an Eskimo in a blinding snowstorm. Put it this way, man—underwear is an accessory that just gets in the way."

"I'm in," Dante said.

"Okay, man, get your beauty rest. Party starts after midnight. If we show up before then, we'll end up mixing with the tourists."

"And what's wrong with that?" Dante cracked. "Maybe

you could hook up with a respectable young lady for a change."

"I've tried that," Max said. "And trust me—there's no bigger freak than a girl who's ditched her church group. I prefer women who openly advertise their slut factor."

Dante laughed. "Are the girls coming?"

"Pippa's in, but Vanity's got a morning photo shoot at sunrise. Not sure about Christina. Her mother was all over the news yesterday screaming about gay kids ruining America. JAP girl's probably in a psych ward somewhere. I sure as hell would be."

"What's up with that?" Dante wondered aloud. "Her mom's coming off like a Malcolm X for the antigay crowd."

"I don't get it, man. I've lived in Miami long enough to get a read on its problems. Shit, there are plenty to throw your weight behind. But I've never thought boys who know the lyrics to every Kylie Minogue song was one of them."

Dante laughed again. "I hear you, man."

"Hey, how's Omar's duct tape repair job working out? Can you still drive that piece of shit?"

"Yeah, man, I'm still rolling," Dante said.

"Good. Later, barrio boy." Max hung up.

Dante stepped into the living room. For a moment, he just stood there quietly, observing his mother, who was watching the overly dramatic *telenovela* unfold with a strange detachment. Usually these shows provided her a great, perhaps singular, joy, her delight in their sweeping emotions and twisting plots palpable on most evenings. But not this one.

Dante zeroed in on the twenty-inch TV with the cracked speaker and fading picture. His mother deserved more. It seemed so unfair, her settling for this shit while the Biaggis had televisions in guest rooms that were bigger, better, and never used.

"We should get a new TV," Dante said. "The color tube's about to go on this one."

"It's fine," Vanessa said dismissively. "I can see what's going on."

"Mom, all the colors are dark," Dante argued gently. "It's no fun to watch it that way. Maybe we should open up an account at Best Buy. They have a deal going where—"

Vanessa shook her head, cutting him off. "This TV is good enough for me."

Dante glanced down at the crushed diamond watch blinging on his wrist. Sometimes it made him feel so guilty that he felt the impulse to chuck it into Miami Bay. His mother didn't wear any jewelry at all. Years ago she'd hocked her wedding ring to buy a used car that would get her back and forth to work. Today the only adornment she entertained was a plastic Timex with a stopwatch feature that kept her housekeeping tasks efficiently humming along.

He fingered the ice on the bezel, imagining how much he could get for it and the nice things he could buy for his mother with the windfall. But then he disregarded the notion entirely. That was ghetto logic. This watch didn't represent fast access to a pile of cash. It represented the dream he went to bed with at night and woke up to each morning—becoming a hip-hop star.

And why couldn't it happen to him? Dante heard stories all the time about young artists who one day had a few hundred dollars folded into their pockets and the next day were scratching their heads trying to figure out what to do with a million. That was a problem he wanted to have.

If it came to pass, though, he could see his mother spoiling all the fun. There were sports stars who splurged on expensive homes in rich neighborhoods for their mothers, only to see the houses go uninhabited as the once-poor-always-poor women stubbornly refused to move from their familiar surroundings. Vanessa Medina would be like that.

She despised hip-hop and called it devil's music. Instead of encouraging Dante, she slammed his musical pursuits as immature and constantly badgered him to pick up a trade like his cousin.

Raoul Medina had gone to a strip mall school for one year, earned a certificate, and now worked as a computer tech at Jackson Memorial Hospital. And she acted like he was freaking Bill Gates.

It was hard to hold on to a dream when you had a mother who wasn't in the dreaming business. But no matter how much that chasm separated Dante from Vanessa, he still felt a deep, abiding, and undying connection to her. And he never questioned her love for him.

An aching sadness slowly tore away at him, though, because life had dealt Vanessa such a bad hand. She didn't possess the optimism to want better, more exciting, seemingly impossible things, not for herself and not for her child, either. If Dante hadn't developed—against all odds—the simple luxury of daydreams to occupy his mind and feed his vision of the future . . . Jesus, he didn't even want to think about how broken and miserable he might be.

"I'm going out later, so I think I'll take a nap," Dante said, rubbing his full stomach and stifling a yawn. He leaned over to kiss his mother's rough cheek. "Don't worry if I'm not here when you wake up."

"Where are you going?" Vanessa asked.

Dante paused. She rarely hit him with questions like that. The less she knew, the better she felt. After all, her idea of a frank discussion about sex had been putting a box of condoms in his room when he turned thirteen. "To a club."

"With Vince?"

"No, Max."

Vanessa's lips fell into a hard line of implicit disapproval.

"Vince works all the time," Dante explained. "And his girl just had a baby, so he's strung out. I don't see much of him anymore."

"And Max has all the money and the fancy car," Vanessa said coldly.

"It's not that. He's cool. We get along."

Vanessa's feet flew off the pillows and landed squarely onto the stained carpet. She stood up and turned on Dante, anger blazing from her tired eyes. "I don't like what's happening to you."

The shock of her outburst wiped his face clean of expression. He didn't get this. Most mothers would be happy to hear that their son was spending less time with a friend who'd just knocked up his sixteen-year-old girlfriend and slaved away at a dead-end fast-food job. But his mother was pissed about it.

"You're not rich, son," Vanessa told him bitterly. "You're poor. Stop pretending. It makes me sick how you let these people pay for your private school and fix your car and give you expensive—"

"Wait a minute," Dante cut in hotly. "I applied for that scholarship just like every other student."

Vanessa shook her head at him as if he were a simpleton. "Do you actually believe that? Miss Faith saw your name on the application, and she brought it to me. I said, 'Yes, that's my son,' and she said, 'Thank God, you just saved me from going through the stack.' It was a handout."

Dante didn't know this. But he also didn't care. "So what? I got a break. I had a connection. Big deal. That's how the world works, Mom. That's how people get ahead. Even *rich* people. They get into schools and they get jobs and they get fat contracts with the government because somebody knows somebody. And I should feel guilty or undeserving or something else just because I got a free one-year ride from the Biaggi Family Foundation? Hell no! That's bullshit!"

"Don't speak to me that way!" Vanessa screamed.

"No, don't *think* that way!" Dante screamed back. "Jesus Christ! I know that I'm poor. *We're* poor. But the difference between you and me, Mom, is that you're not just poor at the bank, you're poor in your *mind*." Dante drove his point home by tapping his temples with his index fingers. "Everything is *fine* to you. My old public school is *fine* as long as I get a diploma and don't get shot at. And if I went to a trade college for five minutes, learned how to work on cars, and got a job doing oil changes at Jiffy Lube, well, shit, that'd probably be *fine,* too!"

"Your father talked this way," Vanessa cried, tears welling up, her voice rising. "And he let those navy recruiters talk him into signing up for that stupid war, because when he got out, they were going to pay for his college and he'd get a big job and a new car and a brand-new house! But he didn't get any of that! My stupid husband got killed! And he didn't even have to go over there! I begged him to stay here with me! With his son! I had a feeling, Dante, I had a terrible feeling that something was going to happen to him!"

She was sobbing now, her face buried in her hands, her body shaking with raw emotion.

Dante had never seen his mother break down like this before. It scared the hell out of him. He moved toward her with every intention of providing comfort.

But Vanessa stepped out of reach and just looked at him as she gathered her composure and wiped her eyes. When she spoke, her voice was fragile. "Your father went against my wishes. He trusted those recruiters, about what the government would do for him, about what the government would do for *us* if anything happened. But they didn't do right by this family. And you know that."

Dante strained to hear more. She never talked about his father. But he wanted to know about his dreams, not the aftermath of military bureaucracy. Who did his father want to be? What did he want to do?

"I don't like you working for all these millionaires," Vanessa went on. "This man who gave you that watch—he's rotten to the core. I know this. What's wrong with Tony Roma's? That was a good job, yes?"

Dante managed a rueful grin.

"I don't like what I see at the Biaggi house, either," she continued. "I don't like the time that you're spending with Max. It gives me that feeling again . . . that something terrible is going to happen."

Dante moved in to embrace her.

And this time Vanessa accepted his arms, hugging him as tightly as her strength allowed. The emotion was back in her voice. "You're a good son, Dante. But you're so much like your father that my heart never stops breaking."

His mother had never told him this before, and it explained the sadness that never seemed to leave her. Dante could run up and down the scale of emotions. But crying never came easy.

"Why can't you want simple things?" Vanessa asked.

Dante didn't have an answer. And the tears were in his eyes now.

From: Max

Call me if u hear from Dante. He's MIA.

3:28 am 7/24/05

chapter thirteen

Vanity was doing push-ups on a private little stretch of South Beach. At seven o'clock in the morning. On a Sunday.

Only for Patrick Demarchelier, the so French and so cool photographer behind the lens for the silly what's inside my purse? *InStyle* minifeature.

And silly was the understatement of the century, as there was no purse to speak of in these girl-in-bikini-splashes-in-the-water pictures. Oh, well. Nobody ever said that fashion was logical.

"More jumping, more jumping! Big laughing!" Patrick sang in his funny accent, crouching low in the surf to get the perfect angle of the Vanity St. John-at-sunrise shot.

She played in the sea with little girl abandon, spinning

like a whirlpool, feeling more gorgeous than any woman had a right to feel in a Versace two-piece that revealed this much.

"You make me craaaaazy," Patrick praised. He gestured for his two assistants holding the reflector boards to move in closer. Magic hour sunlight was a precious thing. There were only mere minutes in a day to capture it.

Suddenly, Vanity felt a divine impulse of inspiration, one that would make the magazine photo editor go apeshit and cause the hairstylist and makeup artist to up their daily Xanax dosage.

In the Hasselblad H1D viewfinder, Patrick had his subject in the crosshairs. "Beauuuuutiiiiiful!"

Right now. Do or die. Vanity went for the money shot, the one that would generate deafening creative buzz and give voice to the one-two punch questions: Who cares what's inside her purse? Why isn't she on the cover?

Without warning, Vanity took a deep breath and dove into the ocean. The last thing she heard before going under was the delighted cry of fashion's number one image master.

"Yay!" Patrick squealed.

And then she came up from the deep, knowing this would only work in the moment of one . . . two . . . three . . . *perfection*.

A pro like Demarchelier would be way ahead of the action. Unlike so many photographers who cannonballed every bit of their focus into what they thought they wanted and ignored a model's mundane human frailties, such as needing to blink, squinting in direct sun, or just being uncomfortable in a cool morning sea that sprouted all-over gooseflesh. But Patrick D. got nuance.

Vanity's breasts broke the surface of the water. The vibrant Miami sunbeams shone on her face. She inclined her head toward them, caught their brilliant light, opened her jewel-green eyes, and parted her voluptuous, salt water-wet lips to reveal just a hint of milk-white teeth. And then she held the pose just long enough to matter . . . once . . . twice . . . three times, basking in the super-intensified rays as if her body were sexually powered by solar energy.

"Got it."

Two words. And Demarchelier had spoken them. The shoot was over. He lowered the medium-format camera like a hunter might put down his rifle, flashing her a warm, enormous smile.

The *InStyle* photo editor marched down as if she owned the deed to the beachfront location. "All I have to say is this: *Fabulosity.*"

Patrick nodded politely at the adult woman with braces who looked like a vaguely pretty baby-sitter.

Vanity emerged from the water, shivering in the wind. "Oh my God—it's freeeeezing!" She laughed as her teeth began to chatter.

Kris, the shoot's stylist, a cute, gay Asian boy with personality for days, dashed over to wrap a white terry-cloth robe around her shoulders. "Walk off with that bikini on, honey, and I'm *so* fired. They're getting *very* stingy about these things."

Using a bedsheet as a makeshift curtain to offer modesty while she changed, Kris entertained Vanity with gossip about stars who stole wardrobe items from photo shoots. Meanwhile, she slipped off the Versace and pulled on Active Cat by Puma, a bike shorts and tank set infused with a ginseng scent to simultaneously calm and energize.

Vanity was just relishing those aromatherapeutic benefits when Mimi rushed to her side. "You sneaky little bitch. I think you gave the hairstylist a panic attack. Nobody expected you to get *all wet.*"

"It was instinct," Vanity said.

"It was *brilliant,*" Mimi countered. "That's what it was. Something big will come of this. I don't know exactly what yet—maybe L'Oréal."

Patrick stepped over to give her a warm hug, kissing both cheeks in that charming European way. "It was a pleasure. You're truly beautiful. How old are you?"

"She's *seventeen!*" Mimi exploded, barging in on their exchange with no apology. "And if the entire male eighteen-to-thirty-four demo hasn't gone blind by now, then they will after they take these pictures into the bathroom!"

Patrick roared with laughter.

"Ew!" Vanity screeched, covering her face in a pantomime of pseudo-disgust over the vile image. The truth was, she hated the wet dream icon factory. But that was the dance in today's media. A famous hot girl needed *InStyle* one month and *Maxim* the next to keep up with the rhythm of the celebrity beat.

Everybody hugged and sweet-talked their good-byes.

As the crew gathered up their equipment and trudged off in the sand, Vanity meandered down to the shoreline and stared out at the glassy sea, marveling at its tranquil beauty. The water, seemingly so cold just minutes ago, felt as warm as baby's milk now as it rushed over her bare feet.

"Are you coming?" Mimi called out from ten feet away.

Vanity shook her head. "Not yet. I think I'll take a walk along the beach."

Mimi skipped down with Vanity's pink Nalgene bottle in hand. "Then you might want this."

Gratefully, Vanity reclaimed the green tea. She guzzled no fewer than eight glasses a day.

"I'd tag along, but there are Katee K fires to put out," Mimi said wearily. "Everybody wants the first interview with mother and daughter. And there's an Internet rumor going around that Katee's really eighteen and will be tried as an adult."

Vanity took in a sharp breath.

But then Mimi rolled her eyes. "Don't get excited. The birth certificate that showed up on The Smoking Gun was a very convincing fake. Who cares, though? Lions Gate wants her for a remake of *Slumber Party Massacre,* and her CD is selling like gangbusters. Next week it's back at number one."

"How's her mother?" Vanity asked.

"Recovered and holding out for millions on the movie deal." Mimi inspected a nail. "If things continue to go *this* well, I might recommend that *you* stab a parent."

Vanity smiled, digging into her Kooba slouch bag for her iPod. "Even if things go south with Katee's career, I'm still open to that idea." She started singing Katee K's hit, "Some Girl Said."

Mimi grinned. "Uh, right words, wrong melody. You're singing 'Wake Up' by Hilary Duff." One beat. "Freudian slip?"

"Oh, not here, dear," Vanity trilled, realizing that Mimi could bring out the inner bitch in anybody. "But Mama Duff better hope big girl Haylie doesn't keep up with current events. She might grab a kitchen knife just to find a real career."

Mimi laughed so hard that she snorted like a pig. "Oh, you are *bad*!"

Vanity airily waved off the mock scolding and started down the beach. Within footsteps, she felt no less than a million miles away, listening to Liz Phair's "Everything to Me."

For the first time in a long time, Vanity sensed a strong, grounded attitude about herself. The shoot had gone fabulously well. Probably because she'd done the responsible thing and prepared for it properly—with plenty of sleep and no alcohol. Imagine that.

Max had pressed hard to get her to join the Mansion brigade last night, but Vanity had successfully resisted, having come to the conclusion—with the help of Dr. Parker—that the most dangerous factor in most situations is your own personality. It was a heady realization.

But it helped put her on a healthier path. For instance, she'd sworn off meaningless hookups. Since that foggy encounter with J.J. at the Surfcomber, Vanity hadn't so much as kissed a guy. Hmm. Perhaps that qualified her to be reconsidered for virgin status. Ha!

Another telling change was the slow development of female friendships. As it turns out, Christina was a fresh and welcome presence—sweet, insightful, loyal, and, oh God, *phenomenally* talented. The way she concentrated on her art with such tireless devotion inspired Vanity to seek out something to call her own. She still didn't know what that would be, but for starters, she took assignments like the Demarchelier shoot seriously, showing up on time and rested as opposed to late and still recovering from a night of partying.

Even Pippa—with all of her attendant money woes—had become more than tolerable. In fact, the British doll could be a blast—always upbeat, funny, and happy to be with friends. It'd become impossible to dislike her, and Vanity had thawed out on the issue of paying Pippa's way. After all, it was only cash. Besides, she had plenty of it. Why be tightfisted?

All of a sudden, Vanity stopped, noticing something odd just ahead. She focused her gaze, making out a lifeless body in the sawgrass of the dunes. Probably a drunken casualty of the take-no-prisoners South Beach party gauntlet.

Curious, she stepped closer, if only to make sure that the idiot was still breathing. And then her heart leaped around in her chest when she realized that the unconscious figure was no stranger. It was Dante Medina!

For a moment, she watched him sleep, peaceful on the quiet beach. Oh God, who was she kidding? Time was supposed to kill a crush. Well, it hadn't. Not this one anyway. Weeks still felt like yesterday. She remembered the first time she'd ever seen him—playing live party boy in front of Black Sand. Now here he was again—playing a dead version of the same on white sand. So much for progress.

"Dante!" She prodded him awake with her foot.

Groggily, he stirred.

"Rough night?"

Dante opened his eyes to discover that he was fully clothed and passed out on the beach. "What the hell?" It killed him to talk. He did so through chapped lips, his voice sounding nothing less than five-years-of-crazy-nights raspy.

"God, what are you doing out here?" Vanity asked. "I got a text from Max. He's looking for you."

Still somewhat disoriented, Dante scanned the general

area and vaguely checked his pockets. "I guest I lost my phone."

"Not to mention your dignity."

Dante struggled to stand up, then massaged his neck with one hand, as if working out a crimp.

Vanity tried not to notice the impressive pop of his bicep. "Shit."

She didn't know whether he was commenting on the embarrassing circumstances or if that was just his general take on life at the moment.

"Do you remember how you got here?" Vanity asked.

He rubbed his eyes. "Not really." One beat. *"Shit."* He patted himself down again, harder this time. And then his left hand clasped his bare right wrist. "I got robbed."

Vanity experienced a tremor of alarm.

"They took everything—my phone, my wallet . . . my watch." He went down on both knees. He buried his face in his hands. At first, she thought he was crying. But it was just one, long agonized moan.

"I don't understand," Vanity said. And she really didn't. "What happened? Did you take some kind of drug?"

Dante stood up, shaking his head. "No . . . I . . . I had this intense thing with my mom. I got a bottle of whiskey, I took a walk on the beach . . . that's the last thing I remember."

"Consider yourself lucky not to be hurt."

"Oh, I'm hurt," Dante argued quietly.

"I mean physically," Vanity maintained earnestly. "You could've been beaten and left for dead."

"I want to kick my own ass right now. Whoever did this could've at least saved me the trouble." His voice got caught on the last bit.

Vanity tugged at his strong arm, gently pulling him away from the dune. "Come on. I'll take you back to my house. You can shower there, and we'll figure out what to do next."

He hesitated.

"Nobody's there," Vanity assured him. "Lala has the twins in Orlando, and my father's in L.A. on business. He won't be back until tomorrow."

In the steamy St. John shower, Dante just collapsed against the wall as the water jets rained down.

No phone.

No wallet.

No watch.

He winced as the terrible reality began to take shape in his troubled mind: No ice. Just gone. No bling. That quick. No diamonds. That automatic.

Robotically, he shut off the spray and wrapped a towel around his waist, trying to stop himself from adding up the damage over and over again. All it did was provide slow torture. But maybe that's what he deserved.

He stepped into Vanity's bedroom. In terms of hotness, the girl was off the centigrade scale, and this is where she slept at night. Yet he felt nothing, no exotic, erotic thrill, just the dull, listless fog of magnificent regret.

"Do you feel better?" Vanity asked.

"I feel worse," Dante admitted. "It's actually starting to sink in now."

"They're just things," Vanity said reasonably. "It's *stuff*. You can replace it. At least you're safe."

Dante glanced around the room that was chockablock full of state-of-the-art electronics, expensive clothes, and pricey accessories. "*You* can replace things. I'm shit out of luck."

Vanity just stood there, as if not knowing what to say.

Dante knew that they were worlds apart on the economic front. Rich girl. Poor boy. But those were old barriers of class. What about the emotional ones? Was he being fair to her? Were they really so different? On paper, they both came from damaged childhoods. His first instinct was to make them strangers when they could actually be soul mates. Maybe it wasn't an issue of money. Maybe it was an issue of depth. He was a guy, a guy with a sheer force of will aimed squarely at the eye of the bull, and that didn't leave a lot of room for complexities.

Finally, Vanity spoke. "Had you been conscious enough to fight for that stupid watch, you'd be dead right now."

The sobering point reached him, and Dante sank down onto Vanity's unmade bed. "You're probably right." He sighed. "It wasn't just the watch, though. It's what the watch represented." His voice sounded wrecked.

Vanity opened her mouth to speak, then seemed to think better of it.

"I don't know how to explain it," Dante went on, rubbing his eyes, massaging his temples. "Shit, my head's killing me." He stopped for a moment to let the throbbing subside. "I believe I've got a shot at making it with my music. I *really* believe that. I just need someone to recognize my talent. And there's so much bullshit out there. If you want to do hip-hop, then they expect you to be a player or a hustler or a pimp. But that's not who I am. I didn't have to do whatever to get by. I'm just a boring poor kid who does his schoolwork and works honest jobs and for the most part listens to his mother." He laughed a little. "I've never even gotten a speeding ticket. I'm not going to pretend to be a thug to get somebody's attention. That's not what I want to say." He eased back onto his elbows and yawned out his fatigue and frustration as he arched his back and watched the muscles ripple in his stomach. "To you this will probably sound lame . . . but that watch felt like one step closer to where I want to be. When I wore it, I wasn't just some wannabe with a drum loop and a few rhymes. I felt like I was going somewhere. And I felt like the right people would somehow see that."

Vanity seemed fully engaged in everything that he was saying.

Dante had never really talked to someone this way, baring

his soul, sharing his heart. It was intense. And he wanted it to go on. Usually, his deal with girls was one-dimensional. If they weren't giving him ass, then they needed to go down. Or move on. But Vanity was a whole new world.

"What the hell's going on here?"

Dante spun around quickly to see Simon St. John in the doorway of his daughter's bedroom. If mixed-race boys could turn white, he would've been the color of a hospital sheet.

"Da-Daddy!" Vanity stammered.

"Is this what you do when you think I'm out of town?" he yelled, the veins in his neck bulging at the strain from his outburst.

"It's not what it looks like. He just took a shower. I found him on the beach. He was robbed."

"He *does* the robbing," Simon St. John snapped. "I got a call from his SafeSplash boss. This thief stole jewelry from the Kelleys on Hibiscus Island."

Dante shook his head, looking around for his old clothes. He couldn't do this half-naked. Shit, he couldn't do this at all. So Rob got tired of waiting for his volcano date and decided to have him fired on some bogus charge. Christ! What else could happen to him today?

"Daddy," Vanity pleaded.

But her father cut her off with a savage look. "A working stiff? Come on. That's slutty, Vanity. Even for a girl like you."

Dante's stomach did a nosedive. From a father's mouth, those words were coldhearted. He watched the hurt and shame play out high on Vanity's cheeks, and he wished that he could take it all away.

Simon St. John glowered at him. "Get the hell out of my house. And just try to leave with anything but the rags you came with. Just try. See what happens."

Wordlessly, Dante ducked into the bathroom to pull on his jeans and slip on his shirt.

Vanity stood waiting for him when he walked out. "I'll take you home," she sad quietly.

"He can walk," Simon said.

Vanity iced her father down with a defiant glare. "I'm giving him a ride."

"I said—"

She cut him off midsentence. "I don't care what you said."

"Listen to me. I'm your—"

Vanity held up a hand. "Don't even say it!" she screamed. "Stop kidding yourself. You haven't been a father to me in years."

And with that, Dante followed her out of the house.

There was a time to remain quiet, even when you desperately wanted to say something. Now was one of those times.

Silently, they drove, top down in her Mercedes SL500, sun blazing. With no explanation, she took him to the Miami Beach Marina adjacent to Government Cut.

Dante followed her onto the busy dock and into a private slip where a gleaming Cobalt 343 waited. It was thirty-four feet long and all-white with a single candy red boot stripe.

Whoever owned it had no change left from a quarter of a million.

Vanity started up the Volvo engines. After a five-minute safety cruise, they were in the Atlantic. And that's when she opened it up.

Dante stood by her side, feeling like the girl half of a couple as Vanity leaned into the wheel, the boat barely skimming the surface of the sea as it propelled across the water like a charging arrow in flight.

Impulsively, he reached out to stroke her cheek. In the beginning, it was just a simple gesture, a hurt boy offering affection to a hurt girl. But it became so much more.

There was a flash of pain on Vanity's face, the disturbance of a bad memory still fresh in her mind. Still, she pressed into him, her mouth meeting his, at first just in quiet exploration, then more aggressively. Her tongue was wet, wild, and wonderful. It parted Dante's dry, chapped lips, coating them with delicious moisture.

Now the Cobalt 343 was driving itself.

With a slow, deliberate hand, Vanity eased down on the throttle, never taking her mouth away from Dante's. The delicate engines got quiet. Then more quiet. And suddenly, they stopped altogether.

Dante shut his eyes, panting a little as Vanity reached for his waist to steady herself against him. The weight of her caused him to fall back against the padded leather cockpit.

She landed on top of him, teeth clashing, tongues at war, saliva flowing together. His blood was racing, pulsing, pounding. Exactly where it mattered. And this was only the first kiss.

Dante's chest heaved, his nostrils flared, and he ached for her in a way that made it impossible for him to stop. Deep down, he knew that he should stop. Because this was far beyond a hookup. He could actually fall for this girl. Hell, he already was. It was intense, desperate, and so freaking complicated. But even as he thought this, his hands moved softly over the curve of her ass.

And then Vanity dropped down to her knees . . . so unexpectedly . . . and so exquisitely. She found the snap-button closure of his jeans, and her beautiful mouth lingered there, savoring the anticipation, breathing warm gusts of air onto the straining part of him.

This was his last chance to say no. But raw hunger kicked all good reason out the door. She wanted it. He needed it. And right now Dante didn't care how much craziness had brought them here. Only an insane person would turn back now. So he cradled Vanity's head with one hand, and then he drew down his zipper for her with the other.

When it was over, the stop messages in Dante's mind were suddenly clear again. And like a fool, he chose to give voice to them right away. "I'm sorry."

Vanity gazed up at him, a question in her eyes. On the list

of things boys told her after favors like that, it was clear that "I'm sorry" didn't have a place in the top ten.

"We should've stopped . . . I should've stopped. That was a mistake." Finally, he got the words out.

And then something about the look on Vanity's face told Dante that the worst day of his life wasn't over yet.

From: J.J.

Bad friend or good businessman? Your choice.
Lummus park at 4.

3:18 pm 7/24/05

epilogue

Max waited in Lummus Park.

Under the shade of palms, he watched the inline skaters roll along the winding sidewalk, tanned and hard-bodied, pretty boys and prettier girls.

J.J. saw Max the moment Max saw him.

The struggling poser wore a faded ringer tee that featured a graphic of two beer mugs and the reassuring phrase, TRUST ME . . . I'M AN ALCOHOLIC.

J.J. stopped for a second to admire the departing end of three microskirted models. The look on his face said the sight was almost painful, but in a way that made it hurt so good. He loped over to join Max on the bench, sweet marijuana breath blowing through parted, Blistex-moist lips. "I thought you'd be curious."

The "about what" hung in the air.

Max glanced down at the Sony HDV Handycam balanced on J.J.'s True Religion denim-clad thigh. Suddenly, the rheostat of his interest twisted up. "You didn't say we were going to the movies. I would've brought popcorn."

J.J. grinned, flicked open the tiny SwivelScreen, and hit playback.

The high-definition video was rich in color, vivid in detail, and explosive in content. That face. That body. That fame. Stripping, vamping, and doing all sorts of wonderfully nasty things.

The impact was nearly too much for Max to take. He tried to hide the fact that he needed to swallow. "How did you get this?"

"She was so wasted that she didn't even notice the camera," J.J. said proudly.

Max stewed in the boiling ice of a dilemma deep, dreadful, and destructive. But there was no stopping the brain schemes that had already cranked up.

Private sex tape.

Public fascination.

Major opportunity.

First Pamela Anderson and Tommy Lee. Then Paris Hilton and Rick Salomon. Now Vanity St. John and Jayson James.

J.J. seemed to be reading Max's mind. "I heard that Rick made more than five mil off his Paris vid."

At first, Max didn't speak, even though he knew that every second of his silence only endorsed the conspiracy. But his torment was total. Vanity was his oldest friend. Their history was long and deep—the same schools, the same birthday parties, the same summer camps, the inevitable ill-fated romance, and the easy friendship that followed.

No matter how hard he fought to stay true to all of that, the business potential steamrolled over his personal feelings. This wasn't a poker game to net a few thousand bucks or a warehouse rave to bring in twenty grand. This shit was huge and could pull down *millions*. And he recognized the sadistic irony, too, that the friend who christened him Baby Don would be the sacrificial lamb in his biggest Baby Don deal.

Finally, he dropped the mute routine and gave voice to the obvious potential playing itself out on the three-inch monitor. He just couldn't resist. "Five million is chump change," Max said. "We can make more."

Christina was good at keeping secrets. She was gay and nobody knew it. She was in love and nobody knew that, either.

"Harajuku girls/I'm looking at you girls/You're so original girls/You got the look that makes you stand out."

She sang along to Gwen Stefani, her mind lost in iPod oblivion, her heart pumping hard, her body clinging to wonderful sense memories—the sound of her voice, the smell of her perfume, the smoothness of her skin.

But when would Christina see her again? When would she talk to her again? That's all she really wanted to know. Not having the answers suspended her moods. She seemed to be hovering in a state of perpetual imbalance, preoccupied with thoughts of her with such intensity that it alternately invigorated her and left her completely exhausted.

Maji de!

Christina giggled to herself as the Tokyo-girl slang so naturally came to mind. It was the expression du jour among young Japanese women, used to convey surprise. The English translation was simply, "No, really?"

Christina was creating her own *shojo manga* called *Harmony Girl*.

Maji de!

Christina's mother would kick her out of the house if she knew the things that she thought and felt about a certain girl.

Maji de!

That girl was Vanity St. John.

Maji de!

Yes, Christina was in love with Vanity.

"You don't look twenty-one." The man studied the New York driver's license suspiciously. And then he studied Pippa more suspiciously.

"Give it a go through E-Seek," she challenged. "You'll see that it's real."

Thank God for Max. His skills were so bang-on that she

didn't have to worry about this bloke calling her bluff. Her fake ID would pass any test.

This one had been created with sophisticated computer software, Internet sources, special inks, a shimmering hologram, and data encoding.

A Max Biaggi Jr. forgery could get you past the rope at any Miami club. It could endure police inspection. It could even survive high-tech verification devices. And right now, it would win over the manager of Cheetah, the strip club of choice for Miami's high rollers.

If Tony Soprano ever decided to go through a year on the South Beach Diet and get hair plug implants, then he'd emerge looking like Vinnie Rossetti. The man was mobster-slick with an expensive suit, loads of gold jewelry, and a sexy, dangerous don't-mess-with-me attitude.

Vinnie stared at Pippa.

Pippa stared at Vinnie.

To walk through these doors had taken some serious psyching up. But now Pippa was here—fierce, determined, and unwilling to turn back.

Money made the world go 'round.

Pippa couldn't rely on her mum for spending power. She couldn't count on her friends, either. The responsibility to make the necessary cash for extraordinary living belonged to her. And it was time to start owning up to that reality.

She glanced at the dark surroundings, taking in two long stages, a mahogany bar, a pool table, several private booths, and a mysterious upstairs area with THE LAIR spelled out in big, junglelike letters.

Pippa had the body. She had the moves, too.

"Come back tomorrow," Vinnie said. "I'll put you on-stage."

Now she had the opportunity.

The cruelest part of the humiliation was that Vanity could still taste Dante on her lips as he gave her chapter and verse on why they shouldn't be together.

"I just can't do this . . ."

She was falling.

"Not against your father's wishes . . ."

She was sinking.

"There's too much at stake for me . . ."

She was fading.

In a life that had no shortage of them, this ranked high among her worst boy-girl moments. Way out here on Miami Beach, chivalry was dead in the water.

"Do you have any idea how that makes me feel?" Vanity asked. Her voice rattled with cold anger. And she didn't wait for an answer before thundering on. "To have you say those things to me not five minutes after . . . *that*? Before we even get back to shore? God! I think I'd feel better about it if you just handed me a twenty-dollar bill and said, 'Thanks.'"

Dante's expression look pained. "I didn't want things to go that far."

As the tears started up, so did Vanity's hatred. For Dante. For herself. For the mess that was her life. "And were you thinking this before or after you unzipped your pants?"

Dante glanced back toward the shore. Right now, taking a chance on jumping out and swimming for it seemed to be his preferred method of conflict resolution with her.

But Vanity's mind was obsessing over ways to hurt him. Badly. "Why did I even bother with you?" She spun her rebuke not only with words but with haughty I'm-rich-you're-poor body language. "This morning you were a beach bum. An hour ago you were a thief. Now you're just a loser on the make. Do you actually think my father will *ever* give you the time of day? The only people who get his tap-on-the-shoulder-I'm-going-to-make-you-a-star bit are the unknowns that his A and R people discover. His opinion is this: If you're so convinced of your talent that you're out there stalking music executives, then you probably have no talent. You just have delusions."

Vanity jumped behind the wheel of the Cobalt, roared the engines, and thrust forward on the throttle, the violent impact of takeoff flattening her against the white leather seat.

Sea rushed by. Speed raged on. The boat traveled away from the shore. Sixty miles per hour was now ancient history. It planed across the smooth surf at seventy. And rising.

Vanity shot a look backward.

Dante's hands were white-knuckled on the guardrail as he crawled toward the cockpit, shouting against the whipping wind for her to slow down, real fear living in his eyes.

All Vanity could think about was how worthless Dante had made her feel. Her father had done the same thing. So had J.J. There had been others, too. But right now it was Dante Medina front and center. In the fog of her fury, he transmogrified into every male who'd ever hurt her.

Vanity's next move was a symbolic one. She kicked high and hard with both feet, hitting Dante like a battering ram in the center of his chest. When the force of impact shot him over the side of the speeding Cobalt, she never looked back.

Out of sight.

Out of mind.

Out of her life.

And then Vanity St. John screamed a new world order into the hot Florida breeze: "Don't fuck with me, boys!"

To be continued . . .

MTV Books
proudly presents

a
fast girls,
hot boys
novel

bling addiction
kylie adams

Coming soon in trade paperback from MTV Books

Turn the page for a sneak preview of
Bling Addiction

C razy bitch!"

By the time Dante surfaced to scream out those words, Vanity and the speeding Cobalt were at least a hundred yards gone.

His throat was instantly raw from the vocal cord strain, not to mention the violent intake of salt water. Getting swallowed up by the wake upon entry had given him a cruel taste of the Atlantic.

He tried to assemble his thoughts, but the shock of the situation had barely registered. Struggling to tread water, he fought to keep his head above the surging tide. Jesus Christ, why had he refused to wear a life jacket? Oh, yeah. To be cool. Like that mattered now.

Dante's gaze remained locked onto the Cobalt as the boat

continued to move farther and farther away. He kept expecting it to cut a wide turn and circle back. But now the watercraft was cruising beyond his sight line. A minute went by. And then another. Both made up the longest one hundred and twenty seconds of Dante Medina's life.

He experienced a steadily rising panic, his breath coming in gasping heaves as he eyeballed the distance to shore. The trip back to land was considerable. Vanity had hauled back the throttles and taken them at least two miles out, if not more. Everything in that direction was a blur. It looked like the skyscrapers of Miami Beach had fallen down.

Dante bobbed in the sea, waiting for the sick joke to end. It had to be over any time now. His eyes would get a visual on the returning boat. Or maybe his ears would hear the rumble of the delicate fuel-injection engines. But the fearful moments just stretched on . . . and no sight or sound ever materialized. Shit! How could she just leave him out here in the middle of the freaking ocean?

Look for
Bling Addiction
wherever books are sold.
Coming soon in trade paperback
from MTV Books.

Dear Readers,

I hope you enjoyed the first book in my new Fast Girls, Hot Boys miniseries. Writing *Cruel Summer* was like crashing a wild party—I had no idea what was going to happen with Vanity, Dante, Max, Pippa, and Christina. In a crazy way, these characters took over and wrote their own story!

At the end of the day, my goal is to offer a book that takes you on a fun, page-turning trip, but sometimes characters go through issues that strike a serious chord, like Vanity's problems with depression.

If you're experiencing similar feelings of stress, sadness, a sense of unworthiness, mood changes, and/or difficulty with relationships, it's important to talk about your problems with someone you can trust. And if those feelings persist, it's equally important to dig deep and find the motivation to ask for help.

One way to get control of overwhelming thoughts and feelings before they get control of you might be to create an Emotional First-Aid Kit. This is a great concept dreamed up by Dr. Lisa Machoian, a former Harvard University researcher and lecturer. You can learn more about her at www.DisappearingGirl.com.

Making your own Emotional First-Aid Kit is easy. First, find a special keepsake box or decorate any kind of box with a photo collage or colorful paints. Next, fill the box with things that make you happy and make you feel good about yourself—pictures of family, friends, and pets, a CD burned with a mix of your favorite songs, personal lists of books, movies, TV shows, websites, photos of celebrities that you love, a small vial of calming aromatherapy oil, a tension-relieving squeeze ball or toy, basically any number of objects or memories to ease you through those pressure-filled moments that can sometimes make a situation seem worse than it actually is.

Do I sound like a school counselor on one of those Lifetime movies? I hope not! I really think the idea of the Emotional First-Aid Kit is a fantastic concept. Just the process of creating it can be therapeutic. And when problems seem almost unbearable, the box itself can be an instant reminder of all the wonderful things about yourself and your life.

Okay, enough Oprah talk! On to some fun stuff. Since I

left you hanging with Vanity, Dante, Max, Pippa, and Christina in various stages of danger and intrigue, it's only fair to tell you that all of those cliff-hangers will be resolved in August with the release of my second Fast Girls, Hot Boys novel. It's called *Bling Addiction,* and it's even more shocking and outrageous than *Cruel Summer*!

In the meantime, I want to invite you to visit my official website at www.readkylie.com for free Fast Girls, Hot Boys reader extras. The first is an exclusive three-part short story called "Jailbait," which is a Fast Girls, Hot Boys prequel focusing on Max's baby sister, Shoshanna. I think you'll enjoy finding out what happens on the weekend of Shoshanna's fifteenth birthday. It's anything but a cake-and-ice-cream affair. This girl is the ultimate wild child!

The second extra is a free Podcast available for immediate download on iTunes. This multisegment radio show is packed with a few spoilers on *Bling Addiction,* cool information about Miami, plus dish on the latest fashion and trends. Just log on to iTunes and type "Fast Girls, Hot Boys" into the Podcast search engine. At no charge you can download the program and subscribe to future Podcasts. There's also a *Cruel Summer* iMix available on iTunes. Just log on and type "Cruel Summer" into the iMix search engine. You'll see a fun playlist featuring songs and artists mentioned in the book. Sort of a sound track to the lives of Vanity, Dante, Max, Pippa, and Christina.

And that's not all! On my website, take a moment to join

the K-List, otherwise known as "Kylie's Inner Circle." There's a special sign-up tab for fans of Fast Girls, Hot Boys. I'll be sending out periodic e-mails on the miniseries, future writing projects, and site updates. And don't forget to post me a K-mail. I love hearing from readers. After all, I'm anxious to find out what you think about *Cruel Summer*!

With all good wishes,

Kylie Adams
www.readkylie.com